WHOSO PULLETH OUTE THIS SWERD OF THIS STONE
IS RIGHTWYS KYNGE BORNE OF ALL BRYTAYGNE

Slowly the king read aloud, tracing the letters in the stone. When he had finished, he looked up at the mage. "But I am king of all Britain."

"Then pull the sword, sire."

The king smiled, and it was not a pleasant smile. He put his hand to the hilt, tightened his fingers around it until the knuckles were white, and pulled.

The sword remained in the stone....

"Like the true bard that she is, Jane Yolen brings home the wild wood of the past to the twentieth century. The images are clean and clear, always pleasing, often kind—never tamed."

—Tanith Lee

"Jane Yolen is one of our genre's few genuine poets, not only a writer but a *storyteller*—as her poem of that title distinguishes the magic from the mundane. She makes the difficult seem effortless."

—Parke Godwin

"This is certainly one of the most important handlings of an old story which has been done recently . . . Ms. Yolen's work is always notable. Here is some of her brightest devising which will be eagerly sought by all those interested in 'The Matter of Britain.'"

—Andre Norton

MERLIN'S BOOKE

JANE YOLEN

THIRTEEN STORIES AND POEMS ABOUT THE ARCH-MAGE

ACE FANTASY BOOKS
NEW YORK

MERLIN'S BOOKE

An Ace Fantasy Book/published by arrangement with
the author

PRINTING HISTORY
Ace Fantasy edition/May 1986

For information address: The Berkley Publishing Group,
200 Madison Avenue, New York, New York 10016.

ISBN: 0-441-52552-0

Ace Fantasy Books are published by The Berkley Publishing Group,
200 Madison Avenue, New York, New York 10016.
PRINTED IN THE UNITED STATES OF AMERICA

Acknowledgments

"The Ballad of the Mage's Birth" copyright © 1986 by Jane Yolen. First publication.

"The Confession of Brother Blaise" copyright © 1986 by Jane Yolen. First publication.

"The Wild Child" copyright © 1986 by Jane Yolen. First publication.

"Dream Reader" copyright © 1986 by Jane Yolen. First publication.

"The Annunciation" copyright © 1985 by Jane Yolen. First published in *Star*Line*, Science Fiction Poetry Association.

"The Gwynhfar" copyright © 1983 by Jane Yolen. First published in TALES OF WONDER (Shocken Books).

"The Dragon's Boy" copyright © 1985 by Jane Yolen. First published in *The Magazine of Fantasy and Science Fiction* (Mercury Press).

"The Sword and the Stone" copyright © 1985 by Jane Yolen. First published in *The Magazine of Fantasy and Science Fiction* (Mercury Press).

"Merlin at Stonehenge" copyright © 1985 by Jane Yolen. First published in *Star*Line*, Science Fiction Poetry Association.

"Evian Steel" copyright © 1985 by Jane Yolen. First published in IMAGINARY LANDS, edited by Robin McKinley (Ace Fantasy Books).

"In the Whitethorn Wood" copyright © 1984 by Jane Yolen. First published in THE WHITETHORN WOOD AND OTHER TALES (Triskell Press).

"Epitaph" copyright © 1986 by Jane Yolen. First publication.

"L'Envoi" copyright © 1986 by Jane Yolen. First publication.

For Terri and Mark

And with special thanks to Emma Bull, Father Robert Coonan, John Crowley, Charles de Lint, Ed Ferman, Bob Frazier, Dr. Justina Gregory, Dr. Vernon Harward, Zane Kotker, Patricia Mac-Lachlan, Robin McKinley, Shulamith Oppenheim, Ann Turner, Will Shetterly, Susan Shwartz, Andrew Sigel, all of whom played some part in the magic show, and especially and always for the arch-mage himself, David Stemple.

Contents

Introduction
Hic Jacet Merlinnus

· When the Glastonbury tomb reputed to belong to Arthur and Guenevere was opened in the twelfth century by impecunious monks, only bones remained in the strong oak casket. That tomb—marked HIC JACET SEPULTUS INCLITUS REX ARTHURIUS IN INSULA AVALONIA, if you believe the seventeenth century antiquary Camden or HIC JACET ARTHURUS, REX QUONDAM, REXQUE FUTURUS if you favor Sir Thomas Malory—was long a favorite touchstone of the pseudo-scholars. And, so the legend continued, alongside the bones was a tress of braided hair *yellow as golde* which, as soon as it was touched, turned to dust.

No tomb for the mage Merlin or Myrddin has ever been found.

Still the figure of the shape-changer, Druid high priest, wizard *extraordinaire,* counselor to kings bestrides the story of Arthur and his court like a colossus. Merlin's own part in the legendary history is culled from sources as diverse as Malory; the thirteenth century Burgundian poet Robert de Boron; the scholar Geoffrey of Monmouth of twelfth century Oxford; Nennius; Wace; a variety of folktales from Scotland, Wales, Ireland, France; and bits that have traveled from as far away as India and Jerusalem. That history begins with a strange birth in a nunnery, continues through Merlin's childhood talents as a seer for King Vortigern, through the tales of a wild, mad Welshman living in the wood of Celyddon, through the troubling prophesies sometimes credited to Nostradamus, and ends in an enchanted sleep in the forest of Broceliande. In between the folk mind has gifted the mage with powers to move stones and to transform a rough, bearish military commander into a great good king of Christendom.

Merlin's greatest power, though, is that centuries of listeners and readers have believed in him. They believed in Geoffrey of Monmouth's version, in Sir Thomas Malory's version, in T.H. White's version, in Mary Stewart's version—even though the Merlin in each of these and hundreds of other recreations is never the same. But then was not Merlin a shape-shifter, a man of shadows, a son of an incubus, a creature of mists? There is not one Merlin, but a multitude, some dark, some light, some mystical and some substantial. Merlin is our magic mirror.

And so you have in your hands a book in which Merlin wears many faces and shapes. He is set in no one time and walks through a landscape now real, now unreal. This is revisionist mythology, stories and poems I wrote over a period of almost five years.

It is important to remember that the only thing to link these stories is the figure of Merlin and he is a different character in each tale. This is not a novel but a series of stories, each looking in toward the mage. But whether it is Merlin as seen through the eyes of the priest who baptized him in "The Confession of Brother Blaise" or through the cynical eyes of a minstrel who recreates the tale in "The Gwynhfar" or through the amnesiac eyes of the feral boy in "The Wild Child," or through the rheumy eyes of the old magician beguiled and ensorceled in the tree in "In the Whitethorn Wood," or through a reporter's notes in "Epitaph," it is the arch-mage seen, as he has always been seen, through a storyteller's eyes, a dreamer's eyes.

The facts about Merlin are few, the spyglass of history being both corrupted and purified by its mythic lens. Yes, there were priests and seers, shanachies and wizards, counselors of war and teachers of Latin in the times past. And some of them may have actually been involved with The Matter of Britain. But what is actual is not necessarily what is true. Merlin was all of these—priest, seer, shanachie, wizard, counselor, and teacher. And he was none of them. He is rather a character touched by fancy. And:

> *Tell me where is fancy bred,*
> *Or in the heart or in the head?*

The answer is, of course, both.

Jane Yolen
Phoenix Farm
Hatfield, Massachusetts
1986

"Many of those who shall read this book or shall hear it read will be the better for it, and will be on their guard against sin."

—the infant Merlin to his confessor, Father Blaise in Vita Merlini by Geoffrey of Monmouth

The Ballad
of the Mage's Birth

The maiden sits upon the stair,
   (The power's in the stone)
And births a son twixt earth and air,
   (Touch magic, pass it on.)

And at her feet a burning tree,
   (The magic's in the stone)
That is as green as green can be,
   (Touch magic, pass it on).

And at her back a mossy well,
   (The glory's in the stone)
For water does complete the spell,
   (Touch magic, pass it on).

Earth, air, fire, water—*words*—
   (The naming's in the stone)
Attend the infant mage's birth,
   (Touch magic, pass it on).

She leaves him there, still bright with blood,
   (The dying's in the stone)
Hard by the green and burning wood,
   (Touch magic, pass it on).

"On my faith," said she, "I know now. Only daughter was I to the king of Demetia. And when still young, I was made a nun in the church of Peter in Carmarthen. And as I slept among my sisters, in my sleep I saw a young man who embraced me; but when I awoke, there was no one but my sisters and myself. After this I conceived and when it pleased God the boy you see there was born. And on my faith in God, more than this never was between a man and myself."

—Historia Regum Britanniae
by Geoffrey of Monmouth

The
Confession of
Brother Blaise

Osney Monastery, January 13, 1125

The slap of sandals along the stone floor was the abbot's first warning.

"It is Brother Blaise." The breathless news preceded the monk's entrance as well. When he finally appeared, his beardless cheeks were pink both from the run and the January chill. "Brother Geoffrey says that Brother Blaise's time has come." The novice breathed deeply of the wood scent in the abbot's parlor and then, because of the importance of his message, he added the unthinkable. *"Hurry!"*

It was to the abbot's everlasting glory that he did not

scold the novice for issuing an order to the monastery's head as a cruder man might have done. Rather, he nodded and turned to gather up what he would need: the cruse of oil, his stole, the book of prayers. He had kept them near him all through the day, just in case. But he marked the boy's offense in the great register of his mind. It was said at Osney that Abbot Walter never forgot a thing. And that he never smiled.

They walked quickly across the snow-dusted courtyard. In the summer those same whitened borders blossomed with herbs and berry bushes, adding a minor touch of beauty to the ugly stone building squatting in the path before them.

The abbot bit his lower lip. So many of the brothers with whom he had shared the past fifty years were housed there now, in the stark infirmary. Brother Stephen, once his prior, had lain all winter with a terrible wasting cough. Brother Homily, who had been the gentlest master of boys and novices imaginable, sat in a cushioned chair blind and going deaf. And dear simple Brother Peter-Paul, whose natural goodness had often put the abbot to shame, no longer recognized any of them and sometimes ran out into the snow without so much as a light summer cassock between his skin and the winter wind. Three others had died just within the year gone by, each a lasting and horrible death. He missed every one of them dreadfully. The worst, he guessed, was at prime.

The younger monks seemed almost foreign to him, untutored somehow, though by that he did not mean they lacked vocation. And the infant oblates—there were five of them ranging in ages from eight to fourteen, given to the abbey by their parents—he loved them as a father should. He did not stint in his affection. But why did he feel this terrible impatience, this lack of charity toward the young? God may have written that a child would lead, but to Abbot Walter's certain knowledge none had led *him*. The ones he truly loved were the men of his own age with whom he had shared so much, from whom he had learned so much. And it was those men who were all so ill and languishing, as if God wanted to punish him by punishing them. Only how could he believe in a God who would do such a thing?

Until yesterday only he and Brother Blaise of the older

monks still held on to any measure of health. He discounted the aching in his bones that presaged any winter storms. And then suddenly, before compline, Blaise had collapsed. Hard work and prayer, whatever the conventional wisdom, broke more good men than it healed.

The abbot suddenly remembered a painting he had seen in a French monastery the one time he had visited the Continent. He had not thought of it in years. It represented a dead woman wrapped in her shroud, her head elaborately dressed. Great white worms gnawed at her bowels. The inscription had shocked him at the time: *Une fois sur toute femme belle* ... Once I was beautiful above all women. But by death I became like this. My flesh was very beautiful, fresh and soft. Now it is altogether turned to ashes. ... It was not the ashes that had appalled him but the worms, gnawing the private part he had only then come to love. He had not touched a woman since. And that Blaise, the patrician of the abbey, would be gnawed soon by those same worms did not bear thinking about. God was very careless with his few treasures.

With a shudder, Abbot Walter pushed the apostasy from his mind. The Devil had been getting to him more and more of late. Cynicism was Satan's first line of offense. And then despair. *Despair*. He sighed.

"Open the door, my son," Abbot Walter said putting it in his gentlest voice, "my hands are quite full."

Like the dortoir, the infirmary was a series of cells off a long, dark hall. Because it was January, all the buildings were cold, damp, and from late afternoon on, lit by small flickering lamps. The shadows that danced along the wall when they passed seemed mocking. *The dance of death,* the abbot thought, *should be a solemn stately measure, not this obscene capering Morris along the stones.*

They turned into the misericorde. There was a roaring fire in the hearth and lamps on each of the bedside tables. The hard bed, the stool beside it, the stark cross on the wall, each cast shadows. Only the man in the bed seemed shadowless. He was the stillest thing in the room.

Abbot Walter walked over to the bed and sat down heavily on the stool. He stared at Blaise and noticed, with a kind of relief crossed with dread, that the man's eyes moved restlessly under the lids.

"He is still alive," whispered the abbot.

"Yes, but not, I fear, for long. That is why I sent for you." The infirmarer, Brother Geoffrey, moved suddenly into the center of the room like a dancer on quiet, subtle feet. "My presence seems to disturb him, as if he were a messenger who has not yet delivered his charge. Only when I observe from a far corner is he quiet."

No sooner had Geoffrey spoken than the still body moved and, with a sudden jerk, a clawlike hand reached out for the abbot's sleeve.

"Walter." Brother Blaise's voice was ragged.

"I will get him water," said the novice, eager to be *doing* something.

"No, my son. He is merely addressing me by name," said the abbot. "But I would have you go into the hall now and wait upon us. Or visit with the others. Your company should cheer them, and a man's final confession and the viaticum is between himself and his priest." The abbot knew this particular boy was prone to homesickness and nightmares and had more than once wakened the monastery hours after midnight with his cries. Better he was absent at the moment of Blaise's death.

The novice left at once, closing the door softly. Geoffrey, too, started out.

"Let Geoffrey stay," Blaise cried out.

Abbot Walter put his hand to Blaise's forehead. "Hush, my dear friend, and husband your strength."

But Blaise shook the hand off. "The babe himself said to me that it should be writ down."

"The babe?" asked the abbot. "The Christ child?"

"He said, 'Many of those who shall read or shall hear of it will be the better for it, and will be on their guard against sin.'" Blaise stopped, then as if speaking lent him strength he otherwise did not have, he continued. "I was not sure if it was Satan speaking—or God. But *you* will know, Walter. You have an instinct for the Devil."

The abbot made a clicking sound with his tongue, but Blaise did not seem to notice. "Let Geoffrey stay. He is our finest scribe and it must be written down. His is the best hand and the sharpest ear, for all that you keep him laboring here amongst the infirm of mind and bowels."

The abbot set his mouth into a firm line. He was used to being scolded in private by Blaise. He relied on Blaise's judgments, for Blaise had been a black canon of great learning and a prelate in a noble house before suddenly, mysteriously, dedicating himself to the life of a monk. But it was mortifying that Blaise should scold in front of Geoffrey who was a literary popinjay with nothing of a monk's quiet habits of thought. Besides, Geoffrey entertained all manner of heresies, and it was all the abbot could do to keep him from infecting the younger brothers. The assignment to the infirmary was to help him curb such apostatical tendencies. But despite his thoughts, the abbot said nothing. One does not argue with a dying man. Instead he turned and instructed Geoffrey quietly.

"Get you a quill and however much vellum you think you might need from the scriptorium. While you are gone, Brother Blaise and I will start this business of preparing for death." He regretted the cynical tone instantly though it brought a small chuckle from Blaise.

Geoffrey bowed his head meekly, which was the best answer, and was gone.

"And now," Abbot Walter said, turning back to the man on the narrow bed. But Blaise was stiller than before and the pallor of his face was the green-white of a corpse. "Oh, my dear Blaise, and have you left me before I could bless you?" The abbot knelt down by the bedside and took the cold hand in his.

At the touch, Brother Blaise opened his eyes once again. "I am not so easily got rid of, Walter." His lips scarcely moved.

The abbot crossed himself, then sat back on the stool. But he did not loose Blaise's hand. For a moment the hand seemed to warm in his. *Or was it,* the abbot thought suddenly, *that his own hand was losing its life?*

"If you will start, father," Blaise said formally. Then, as if he had lost the thread of his thought for a moment, he stopped. He began again. "Start. And I shall be ready for confession by the time Brother Geoffrey is back." He paused

and smiled, and so thin had his face become overnight it
was as if a skull grinned. "Geoffrey will have a retrimmed
quill and full folio with him, enough for an epic, at least.
He has talent, Walter."

"But not for the monastic life," said the abbot as he kissed
the stole and put it around his neck. "Or even for the priest-
hood."

"Perhaps he will surprise you," said Blaise.

"Nothing Geoffrey does surprises me. Everything he does
is informed by wit instead of wisdom, by facility instead
of faith."

"Then perhaps you will surprise him." Blaise brought
his hands together in prayer and, for a moment, looked like
one of the stone *gisant* carved on a tomb cover. "I am ready,
father."

The opening words of the ritual were a comfort to them
both, a reminder of all they had shared. The sound of Geoffrey opening the door startled the abbot, but Blaise, without
further assurances, began his confession. His voice grew
stronger as he talked.

"If this be a sin, I do heartily repent of it. It happened
over thirty years ago but not a day goes by that I do not
think on it and wonder if what I did then was right or wrong.

"I was confessor to the King of Dayfed and his family,
a living given to me as I was a child of that same king,
though born on the wrong side of the blanket, my mother
being a lesser woman of the queen's.

"I was contented at the king's court for he was kind to
all of his bastards, and we were legion. Of his own legal
children, he had but two, a whining whey-faced son who
even now sits on the throne no better man than he was a
child, and a daughter of surpassing grace."

Blaise began to cough a bit and the abbot slipped a hand
under his back to raise him to a more comfortable position.
The sick man noticed Geoffrey at the desk in the far corner.
"Are you writing all of this down?"

"Yes, brother."

"Read it to me. The last part of it."

" . . . and a daughter of surprising grace."

"*Surpassing.* But never mind, it was surprising, too,
given that her mother was such a shrew. No wonder the

king, my father, turned to other women. But write it as you will, Geoffrey. The words can change as long as alteration does not alter the sense of it."

"You may trust me, Brother Blaise."

"He may—but I do not," said the abbot. "Bring the desk closer to the bed. You will hear better—and have better light as well—and Blaise will not have to strain."

Geoffrey pushed the oak desk into the center of the room where he might closer attend the sick man's words.

When Geoffrey was ready, Blaise began again.

"She was his favorite, little Ellyne, with a slow smile and a mild disposition. Mild disposition? Yes, that was her outer face to the world. But she was also infernally stubborn about those things she held dear.

"She had been promised before birth to the Convent of St. Peter by her mother who had longed for a daughter after bearing the king an heir. All his by-blows had been boys, which made the queen's desire for a daughter even greater.

"When Ellyne was born, the queen repented of her promise at once, for the child was bright and fair. Rings and silver candlesticks and seven cups of beaten gold were sent to the church in her stead. The good sisters were well pleased and did not press for the child.

"But when Ellyne was old enough to speak her own mind, she determined that she would honor her mother's promise. Despite the entreaties of her mother and father and the assurances of the abbess that she need not come, she would not be turned aside from her decision.

"I was, at that time, her confessor as well as the king's. At his request I added my pleas to theirs. I loved her as I loved no other, for she was a beautiful little thing, with a quick mind I feared would be dulled behind the convent walls. It was thought that she would listen to me, her 'Bobba' as she called me, sooner than to another. But the child shamed me, saying, 'Can you, who has turned his life entirely toward God, ask me not to do the same?' It was that question that convinced me that she was right for, you see, I was a priest by convenience and not conviction. Yet when she said it, she set me on the path by her side.

"She entered the convent the very next day."

Blaise paused, and the abbot moistened his mouth with

a cloth dipped in a bowl of scented water that stood on the table. The *scratch, scratch, scratch* of Geoffrey's pen continued into the silence.

"She was eight when she entered and eighteen when the thing came to pass that led me to Osney—and eventually to this room."

Abbot Walter moved closer to the bed.

"I was in my study when the mother superior herself came bursting into the room. Ordinarily she would have sent a messenger for me, but such was her agitation, she came herself, sailing into my study like a great prowed ship under full sail.

"'Father Blaise,' she said, 'you must come to my parlor at once, and alone. Without asking a single question of me yet.'

"I rose, picked up a breviary, and followed her. We used the back stair that was behind a door hidden by an arras. It was not so much secret as unused. But Mother Agnes knew of it and insisted we go that way. As we raced down the steps, dodging skeins of cobwebs, I tried to puzzle out the need for such secrecy and her agitation and fear. Was there a plague amongst the sisters? Had two been found in the occasion of sin? Or had something happened to little Ellyne, now called Sister Martha? Somehow the last was my greatest fear.

"When we arrived in her spare, sweet-scented parlor, there was a sister kneeling in front of the hearth, her back to us, her face uplifted to the crucifix above.

"'Stand, sister,' commanded Mother Agnes.

"The nun stood and turned to face us and my greatest fear was realized. It was Sister Martha, her face shining with tears. There was a flush on her cheeks that could not be explained by the hearth for it was summer and there was no fire in the grate."

Blaise's voice was becoming ragged again, and the abbot offered him a sip of barley water, holding the cup to his mouth. Geoffrey's pen finished the last line and he looked up expectantly.

"When she saw me, Sister Martha began to cry again and ran to me, flinging her arms around me the way she had done as a child.

"'Oh, Bobba,' she cried out, 'I swear I have done nothing, unless sleeping is more than nothing.'

"Mother Agnes raised her head and thrust her chin forward. 'Tell Father Blaise what you told me, child.'

"'On my faith, father, I was asleep in a room several months ago, surrounded by my sisters. Sisters Agatha and Armory were on my right, Sisters Adolfa and Marie on my left. Marie snores. And the door was locked.'

"'From the outside!' said Mother Agnes, nodding her head sharply, like a sword in its downward thrust. 'All the sisters sleep under lock, and I and my prioress hold the only keys.'"

"A barbaric custom," muttered Abbot Walter. "It shows a lack of trust. And, should there be a fire, disastrous."

Blaise coughed violently but after a few more sips of barley water, he was able to go on.

"Ellyne folded her hands before her and continued. 'In my deepest sleep,' she said, looking down as if embarrassed by the memory, 'I dreamed that a young man, clothed in light and as beautiful as the sun, came to my bed and embraced me. His cheeks were rough on mine and he kissed my breasts hard enough to leave marks. Then he pierced me and filled me until I cried out with fear. And delight. But it was only a dream.'

"'Such dreams are disgusting and violate your vows,' spat out Mother Agnes.

"'Now, now, mother,' I interrupted, 'all girls have such dreams, even when they are nuns. Just as the novice monks, before they are purged of the old Adam, often have similar dreams. But surely you did not call me here to confront Ellyne . . . ah, Sister Martha . . . about a bad dream which is, at worst, a minor venial sin.'

"'A bad dream?' Mother Agnes was trembling. 'Then, Father Blaise, what call you *this?*'

"She stripped away the girl's black robe, and Sister Martha stood there in a white shift in which the mark of her pregnancy was unmistakable."

Geoffrey's quill punctuated the sentence with such vehemence that the ink splattered across the page. It took him several minutes to blot the vellum, and the abbot bathed Blaise's brow with water and smoothed down the brychan around his legs until Geoffrey was ready again.

"'I do not understand, Ellsie,' I said to her, in my anger returning to her childhood name.

"'I do not understand either, Father Blaise,' she answered, her voice not quite breaking. 'When I awoke I was in the room still surrounded by my sisters, all of whom slept as soundly as before. And that was how I knew it had been but a dream. On my faith in God, more than this there was never between a man and myself.' She stopped and then added as if the admission proved her innocence, 'I have dreamed of him every night since but he has not again touched me. He just stands at my bed foot and watches.'

"I put my hands behind me and clasped them to keep them from shaking. 'This sort of thing I have heard of, mother. The girl is blameless. She has been set upon by an incubus, the devil who comes in dreams to seduce the innocent.'

"'Well, she carries the other marks she spoke of,' said Mother Agnes. 'The burns on her cheeks you can see for yourself. I will vouch for the rest.' She draped the cloak again over the girl's shoulders almost tenderly, then turned to glare at me. 'An incubus—not a human—you are sure?'

"'I am sure,' I said, though I was not sure at all. Ellyne had been headstrong about certain things, though how a young man might have trysted with her with Mother Agnes her abbess, I could not imagine. 'But in her condition she cannot remain in the convent. Leave her here in your parlor, and I will go at once and speak to the king.'"

Blaise's last word faded and he closed his eyes. The abbot leaned over and, dipping his finger into the oil, made the sign of the cross on Blaise's forehead. *In nomine Patris, et Filii, et Spiritus sancti, exstinguatur in te omnis virtus diaboli per . . .*"

Opening his eyes, Blaise cried out, "I am not done. I swear to you I will not die before I have told it all."

"Then be done with it," said the abbot. He said it quickly but gently.

"Speaking to the king was easy. Speaking to his shrewish wife was not. She screamed and blamed me for letting the girl go into the convent, and her husband for permitting Ellyne to stay. She ranted against men and devils indiscrim-

inately. But when I suggested it would be best for Ellyne
to return to the palace, the queen refused, declaring her
dead.

"And so it was that I fostered her to a couple in Carmarthen who were known to me as a closemouthed, devoted,
and childless pair. They were of yeoman stock, but as Ellyne
had spent the last ten years of her life on the bread, cheese,
and prayers of a convent, she would not find their simple
farm life a burden. And the farm ran on its own canonical
hours: cock's crow, feed time, milking.

"So for the last months of her strange pregnancy, she
was—if not exactly happy—at least content. Whether she
still dreamed of the devil clothed in sunlight, she did not
say. She worked alongside the couple and they loved her
as their own."

Blaise struggled to sit upright in bed.

"Do not fuss," the abbot said. "Geoffrey and I will help
you." He signaled to the infirmarer who stood, quickly
blotting the smudges on his hands along the edges of his
robe. Together they helped settle Blaise into a more comfortable position.

"I am fine now," he said. Then, when Geoffrey was once
more standing at the desk, Blaise began again. "In the ninth
month, for the first time, Ellyne became afraid.

"'Father,' she questioned me day after day, 'will the child
be human? Will it have a heart? Will it bear a soul?'

"And to keep her from sorrow before time, I answered
as deviously as I could without actually telling a lie. 'What
else should it be but human?' I would say. 'You are God's
own; should not your child be the same?' But the truth was
that I did not know. What I read was not reassuring. The
child might be a demon or a barbary ape or anything in-
between.

"Then on the night before All Hallow's, unpropitious
eve, Ellyne's labor began. The water flooded down her legs
and the child's passage rippled across her belly. The farmer
came to my door and said simply, 'It is her time.'

"I took my stole, the oil, a Testament, candles, a crucifix,
and an extra rosary. I vowed I would be prepared for any
eventuality.

"She was well into labor when I arrived. The farm wife

was firm with her but gentle as well, having survived the birth of every calf and kitten on the place. She allowed Ellyne to yell but not to scream, to call out but not to cry. She kept her busy panting like a beast so that the pains of the birth would pass by. It seemed to work, and I learned that there was a rhythm to this, God's greatest mystery: pain, not-pain, over and over and over again.

"Before long the farm wife said, 'Father Blaise, the child, whatever it be, comes.' She pointed—and I looked.

"From between Ellyne's legs, as if climbing out of a blood-filled cave, crawled a child, part human and part imp. It had the most beautiful face, like an ivory carving of an angel, and eyes the blue of Our Lady's robe. The body was perfectly formed. Up over one shoulder lay a strange cord, the tip nestling into the little hollow at its neck. At first I thought the cord was the umbilicus, but when the farm wife went to touch it, the cord uncoiled from the child's neck and slashed at her hand. Then I knew it was a tail.

"The farm wife screamed. The farmer also. I grabbed the babe firmly with my left hand and, dipping my right finger into the holy oil, made the sign of the cross on its forehead, on its belly, on its genitals, and on its feet. Then I turned it over and pinned it with my left forearm, and with my right hand anointed the tail where it joined the buttocks.

"The imp screamed as if in terrible pain and its tail burst into flames, turning in an instant to ash. All that was left was a scar at the top of the buttocks, above the crack.

"I lifted up my left arm and the child rolled over, reaching up with its hands. It was then I saw that it had claws instead of fingers and it scratched me on the top of both my hands, from the mid finger straight down to the line of the wrist. I shouted God's name and almost dropped the holy oil, but miraculously held on. And though I was now bleeding profusely from the wounds, I managed somehow to capture both those sharp claws in my left hand and with my right anoint the imp's hands. The child screamed again and, as I watched, the imp aspect disappeared completely, the claws fell off to reveal two perfectly formed hands, and the child was suddenly and wholly human."

Blaise had become so agitated during this recitation that the bed itself began to shake. Geoffrey had to leave off

writing and come over to help the abbot calm him. They
soothed his head and the abbot whispered, "Where is the
sin in all this, Blaise?"

The monk's eyes blinked and with an effort Blaise calmed
himself. "The sin?" His voice cracked. Tears began to course
down his cheeks. "The sin was not in baptizing the babe.
That was godly work. But what came after—was it a sin
or not? I do not know, for the child spoke to me. *Spoke*."

"A newborn cannot speak," said Geoffrey.

"*Jesu!* Do you think I do not know that? But this one
did. He said, '*Holy, holy, holy,*' and the words shot from
his mouth in gouts of flame. 'You shall write this down,
my uncle,' he said, 'Write down that my mother, your half
sister, was sinless. That her son shall save a small part of
the world. That I shall be prophet and mage, lawgiver and
lawbreaker, king of the unseen worlds and counselor to those
seen. I shall die and I shall live, in the past and in the future
also. Many of those who shall read what you write or who
shall hear it read will be the better for it and will be on their
guard against sin.' And then the flames died down and the
babe put its finger in its mouth to suck on it like any newborn
and did not speak again. But the sin of it is that I did *not*
write it down, nor even speak of it save to you now in this
last hour, for I thought it the devil tempting me."

Abbot Walter was silent for a moment. *It was so much
easier,* he thought, *for a man to believe in the Devil than
in God.* Then he reached over and smoothed the covers
across Brother Blaise's chest. "Did the farmer or his wife
hear the child speak?"

"No," whispered Blaise hoarsely, "for when the tail struck
the woman's hand, they both bolted from the room in fear."

"And Ellyne?"

"She was near to death from blood loss and heard nothing." Blaise closed his eyes.

Abbot Walter cleared his throat. "You have done only
what you believed right, Blaise. I shall think more on this.
But as for you, you may let go of your earthly life knowing
that you shall have absolution, that you have done nothing
sinful to keep you from God's Heaven." He anointed the
paper-thin eyelids. "*Per sitam sanctam Unctionem, et suam*

piissimam misericordiam, indulgeat tibi Dominus quid quid per visum deliquisti. Amen."

"Amen," echoed Geoffrey.

The abbot added the signs over the nose and mouth, and Blaise murmured in Latin along with him. Then, as the abbot dipped his fingers once more into the jar of oil, Geoffrey took Blaise's hands in his and lay them with great gentleness side by side on top of the covers, and gasped.

"Look, father."

Abbot Walter followed Geoffrey's pointing finger. On the back of each of Blaise's hands was a single, long, ridged scar starting at the middle finger and running down to the wrist. The abbot crossed himself hastily, getting oil on the front of his habit. *"Jesu!"* he breathed out. Until that moment he had not quite believed Blaise's story. Over the years he had discovered that old men and dying men sometimes make merry with the truth.

Geoffrey backed away to the safety of his desk and crossed himself twice, just to be sure.

With deliberate slowness, the abbot put his fingers back into the oil and with great care anointed Blaise's hands along the line of the scar, then slashed across, careful to enunciate every syllable of the prayer. When he reached the end, *". . . quid quid per tactum deliquisiti. Amen,"* the oil on Blaise's skin burst into flames, bright orange with a blue arrow at the heart. As quickly, the flames were gone and a brilliant red wound the shape of a cross opened on each hand. Then, as the abbot and Geoffrey watched, each wound healed to a scab, the scab to a scar, and the scar faded until the skin was clean and whole. With a sigh that seemed a combination of joy and relief, Blaise died.

"In nomine Patris, et Filii, et Spiritus sancti . . ." intoned the abbot. He removed the covers from the corpse and completed the anointing. He felt better than he had all winter, than he had in years, filled with a kind of spiritual buoyancy, like a child's kite that had been suddenly set free into the wind. If there was a Devil, there was also a God. Blaise had died to show him that. He finished the prayers for absolution, but they were only for the form of it. He knew in his inmost heart that the absolution had taken place

already and that Blaise's sinless spirit was fast winging its
way to Heaven. Now it was time to forgive himself his own
sins. He turned to Geoffrey who was standing at the desk.

"Geoffrey, my dear son, you *shall* write this down and
in your own way. Then we will all be the better for it. The
babe, imp or angel, magician or king, was right about that.
Only, perhaps, you should not say just *when* all this happened, for the sake of the Princess Ellyne. Set it in the past,
at such a time when miracles happened with *surprising*
regularity. It is much easier to accept a miracle that has
been approved by time. But you and I shall know when it
took place. You and I—*and God*—will remember."

Surprised, Geoffrey nodded. He wondered what it was
that had so changed the abbot, for he was actually smiling.
And it was said at Osney that Abbot Walter never smiled.
That such a thing had happened would be miracle enough
for the brothers in the monastery. The other miracle, the
one he would write about, *that* one was for the rest of the
world.

"He entered the wood and rejoiced to lie hidden under the ash trees; he marvelled at the wild beasts feeding on the grass of the glades; now he chased after them and again he flew past them; he lived on the roots of grasses and on the grass, on the fruit of the trees and on the mulberries of the thicket. He became a sylvan man just as though devoted to the woods. For a whole summer after this, hidden like a wild animal, he remained buried in the woods, found by no one and forgetful of himself and of his kindred."

— Vita Merlini
by Geoffrey of Monmouth

The
Wild Child

He had been a long time in the wood, and what speech he still had was interspersed with bird song and the grunting warning of the wild boar. He knew his patch of woodland, every bush of it, and had marked it as his own by letting go short streams on the jumbled, over-ground roots of the tallest trees. Oaks were his favorites, though he had his own name for them.

He caught fish by damming up the little stream, bright silvery fish with spotted backs, scarce a hand's span long. And he spied on rabbits and baby squirrels when he could find their hidey-holes, and badgers in their setts. At night he could call down owls. Once he had scared a fox off its kill by growling fiercely but he could not eat the remains. And several times a pack of wild dogs forced him off his own dinner to the safety of a tree. They scattered his cache but did not eat it.

Mostly he existed on mushrooms and sweet roots and grasses and wild berries and raw fish which, by some miracle, never made him sick. He was very thin with knobs for knees and elbows like arrow points and scratches all over his body, which was brown everywhere from the sun. His thatch of straight dark hair fell across his face, often obscuring his woods-green eyes.

He had never made a fire and was even a little afraid to, for he thought fire a poor relation to the lightning that felled trees and left glowing embers over which he had several times roasted his fish. He feared fire, but he did not worship it. If he worshipped anything, it was the trees that sheltered him, fed him, gave him a high resting from the fiercest beasts.

He was eight years old.

The whole time he had lived alone in the woods came to one easy winter, one very wet spring, one mild summer, and one brilliant fall, but for an eight year old that is a good portion of a lifetime. It is certainly a long part of memory. What he could recall of his past life and how he had come to the forest made him uneasy, and he remembered it mostly at night in dreams.

He remembered a smoky hearth and a hand slapping his because he was holding a large joint of meat. However hard he tried, he could not recall who had slapped him. That was not a bad dream though. He remembered the taste of the meat before the slap and it was good.

He remembered sitting atop a great beast, so broad his legs stuck out straight to either side. And he could still feel three or four hands holding him up, steadying him on the animal's back. Each hand had a gold band on the next-to-last finger. And that was a good dream, too. He could still recall the animal's musty smell, especially if the tree he slept in held the memory of its previous occupant strongly.

But the other dreams were bad.

There was the dream of the two dragons, one red and one white, sleeping in hollow stones, who woke when he looked at them. That dream ended horribly in fire, and he could hear the screams of someone being slowly burned to death. The smell was not so different from the smell of the small hare he had found charred under the roots of a lightning-struck tree.

There was the dream of lying within a circle of great stones that danced around him, faster and faster, until they made a blurry gray wall that held him in. Awake, he avoided rocky outcroppings, preferring to sleep in trees rather than in caves. The hollow of an oak was safer than the great, dark, hollow mouths that opened into the hills.

And there was the dream of a man and a sword. Sometimes the man pointed the sword at him, sometimes he held it away. But the sword's blade was like a silvery river in which many wonderful and fearful things swam: dragons, knights on horseback, ladies lying in barges, and the most awful of all, a beautiful woman with long, dark hair and bare arms, who beckoned and sang to him with a mouth that was black and tongueless.

He could not stop the dreams from coming, but he had learned how to force himself to wake before he was caught forever. In the dream, he pushed his hands together, crossed his forefingers, and said his name out loud. Then his eyes would open—his real eyes not his dream eyes—and he would slowly rise up out of the dream and see the leaves of the trees outlined in the light of a pale moon or the stars flickering in their ancient patterns. Only once he was awake he no longer could recall his name.

So he thought of himself as Star Boy or Moon Boy or Boy of the Falling Leaves, whatever caught his fancy or his eye. He did not think of himself in the intimate voice, did not think *I* am or *I* want or *I* will. It was always Star Boy is hungry or Moon Boy wants to sleep or Boy of the Falling Leaves drinks. Time for him was always *now*. As more and more of his words fell away, so did his need for past or future and his only memory was in dreams.

It was the tag-end of fall, and the squirrels had been storing up acorn mast, hiding things in holes, burying and unburying in a frenzied manner. A double V of late geese, noisy and aggravated, flew across the gray and lowering sky. The boy had watched them for a long time, yearning for something he could not quite recall. He shaded his eyes, following their progress until the last one disappeared, a speck behind the mountain. He sighed. Then he squatted and urinated right there in the path, something he never did, his fastidious nature usually forcing him to do such things in the brush. But the geese had awakened in him such a longing that he had forgotten everything for the moment and became as an infant again. Then, suddenly aware of what he had done, he scrabbled around the path, digging with his nails and a stick, loosening enough dirt to cover the wet patch.

Pleased with his concealment, he noticed that his hands were filthy. He checked the sky once more and then turned abruptly, running down the deer track to the river. He plunged in and paddled awkwardly near the edges until he felt clean again. Then he stood a moment more, for the cold water made his skin tingle pleasantly. When he climbed out, he shook himself like a dog and pushed the hair from his eyes.

The geese were gone and yet the memory of that squawking line stayed with him. He wandered off the path to uncover a squirrel's cache of nuts—one of the many he had memorized—and ate each nut slowly, savoring the slightly bitter taste. He hummed as he walked on, a formless little melody that had no words. When he yawned, his hand went to his mouth as if it had a memory of its own. He climbed into a tree, nestled in its crotch, and napped.

A strange noise woke him, but he did not move except to open his eyes. The calling, not yippy like the foxes' or long like the howling fall of the wolves', teased into his dream, and that changed the dream so abruptly, he woke. The calling came closer.

Carefully he unwound himself from the tree crotch and crawled out along a thick branch that overlooked the clearing. Something flapped overhead and he craned his neck. It was a hunting bird; he could see the creamy breast. Her tail was banded with white and brown alternating. Her fierce beak and talons flashed by. She caught an updraft and landed near the top of a tall beech tree.

No sooner had the falcon settled than the calling began again, seeming to invade the clearing.

The boy looked down. On the edge of the wood stood a man, rather like the one with the sword in his dream. He was large, with wide shoulders and hair that covered his face. There was a thin halo of hair around his head. When he walked beneath the branch where the boy lay, the boy could see a round pink area on the top of the man's head that looked like a moon, a spotty pink moon. The boy put a hand to his mouth to keep from laughing aloud.

The man did not notice the boy. His eyes were on the beech and the bird near its crown. He stood respectfully away from the tree and swung a weighted string over his head. But the bird, though it watched him carefully, did not move.

The boy wondered at them both.

The man and the bird eyed one another for the rest of the short afternoon. Occasionally the bird would flutter her wings, as if testing them. Occasionally her head swiveled one way, then the other. But she made no move to leave the beech. The man seemed likewise content to stay. Except for making more circles around his head with the string, he remained motionless, though every now and again he made a chucking sound with his tongue. He talked continuously to the bird, calling her names like "Hinny" and "Love" and "Sweet Nell" and "Bitch," all in that same soft voice.

The boy wondered if the man would attempt to climb the tree after the bird, but he hoped that would not happen. The bird might leave; the tree, quite thin at the top, might break. The boy rather liked the look of the bird: her fierce, sharp independence, the way she stared at the man and then away. And the man's voice was comforting. He hoped they would both stay. At least for a while.

When night came, they each slept where they were: the man right out in the clearing, his hands around his knees; the hawk high up in her tree. The boy edged back down the branch so quietly none of the few remaining leaves slipped off, and nestled into the snug crotch again. He kept his hands warm between his thighs and when he moved just a little, a pleasant feeling went through him. He smiled as he slept though he did not dream.

* * *

In the morning the boy woke first, even before the bird, because he willed himself to. He watched as first the falcon shook herself into awareness, then the man below stretched and stood. The man was about to swing the lure above his head again when the falcon pumped her wings and took off from the tree at a small brown lark, chasing it until they were both almost out of sight.

The boy made slits of his eyes so he could watch, as first one then the other took advantage of the currents of air. It almost seemed, he thought, as if the lark were sometimes chasing the hawk. Seesawing back and forth, the birds flew on, circled suddenly, and headed back toward the clearing. The boy's hands in fists were hard against his chest as he watched, cheering first for the little bird, then for the larger.

Suddenly the lark swooped downward and the falcon hovered for a moment. Only a moment. Then with one long, perilous, vertical stoop, it fell upon the lark and knocked it so hard the little bird tumbled over and over and over till it hit the ground not fifty feet from the man. The falcon, never looking away from the dying bird, followed it to earth. Then it sank its talons into its prey and looked about fiercely.

The man walked quickly but without excess motion to the hawk. He nodded almost imperceptibly at her, knelt, and put one hand on her back and wings while with the other hooded her so swiftly the boy did not even see it till it was done. Then the man stood, placed the bird on his gloved wrist, gathered up the dead lark and the lure with his free hand, and walked smoothly toward the part of the forest where he had come from.

Only when the man had disappeared into the underbrush did the boy unwind himself from the tree. The man, the falcon, the dead bird were all so fascinating, he could not help himself. He *had* to see more. So he ran over to the clearing's edge and, after no more than a moment's hesitation like the falcon hovering, plunged in after them.

The day being mild but somewhat blowy, the clouds ripping across the sky, the boy did not hear as clearly as usual. But the man's path through the underbrush was well marked by broken boughs and the deep impression of his boot heels. He was not hard to follow.

Cautiously at first, then with a kind of eager anticipation, the boy went on. In his eagerness he neglected to note anything about the place, though that in itself was not dangerous as it would be simple enough to find the way back along the same wide, careless swath. The thorny berry bushes scratched his legs, leaving a thin red map from hip to ankle. Once he trod on a nettle. But nothing could dampen his excitement, not even the small prickle of fear he felt. If anything that sharpened it.

Several hours passed like moments, and still the boy remained eagerly on the track. Only twice he had actually glimpsed the man. Once he saw his back, broad and covered with a leathern coat of some sort. *Coat.* That was a word suddenly returned to him. Then he thought, *jerkin*. And the two words, so dissimilar yet peculiarly so much the same, distressed him. He stopped for a minute and said each of them aloud.

"Coat." The word was short, sharp, like a bark.

"Jerkin." He liked that word better and said it over again several more times. "Jerkin, jerkin, jerkin." Then he smiled and looked up. The man was gone.

The boy found the easy trail and followed, running at first to make up the lost time, then settling into a steady walk.

The second time the man turned and looked right at him. The boy froze and willed himself to disappear into the brush the way a new fawn and badgers and even the bright foxes could. It must have worked. The man looked at him but did not seem to see him, stroked the falcon's shoulder once, whispered something the boy could not hear to the bird, then turned away and walked on.

The boy followed but a little more carefully this time, stopping frequently to hide behind a tree or bushes or blend into the dense brush.

He was watching the path so carefully, its having changed from a trail of broken undergrowth to a worn away trail packed down by a succession of feet. He could read the man's faint boot marks, the sharp impressions of deer feet, the softer scrapings of badger, and even the scratchings of grouse. The path and his slow reading of it occupied him and he did not pay attention to what lay ahead. So he was surprised by the turning in the road that opened into a new clearing and by the farmhouse near the center of it.

The farmhouse explained the new scents that he had been ignoring.

As he crept into the clearing and hesitated by the trees, a sudden clamor greeted the man ahead of him. Sharp, excited yips and the chipping and clucking of birds. *Dogs* and *hens*. Those familiar words burst through the boy. "Dogs" and "hens." He mouthed them.

There was a high whinnying from one of the two outbuildings, the one on the left side of the house.

"Horse!" the boy cried out, his own voice reminding him of the size of horses, enormous beasts with soft, broad backs and the smell of home.

He edged closer to the house, sniffing a little as he went, almost drinking in the odors, his chin raised and quivering.

The dogs began barking again and, without meaning to, he shivered and turned to run away.

"Not so fast, youngling," said the man who loomed suddenly by him and grabbed him in two enormous arms, holding him off the ground by the shoulders.

The boy kicked and screamed and tried to slice at the man's face with his nails, but the man dropped him and grabbed both of his hands with almost one motion, prisoning him as deftly as he had the falcon. Then he marched the boy toward the farm, talking all the while in a soft, steady voice.

"Now hush, son, weanling, my young one, my wild one. Hush, you damned little eelkin. I'll wash your face and hair and see what hides under all that mop. Hush, my johnny, my jo." The soft murmuration continued all the way to the house.

"Mag, fetch me a great towel. Nell, my girl, put hot water in the bath. I've caught me a wild thing that followed me all through the wood." The soft voice never got hard, only louder, and two women with kerchiefs binding their heads seemed to spring into being from the fireplace to do the man's bidding.

"Oh, sir," said the girl with the water, her eyes round as

pools, "is it a bogle, all nekkid and brown like that?"

"It is a boy," said the man. "A sharp-eyed, underfed boy not that much older than your own brother Rob. As for naked, he'd not been able to make clothes for himself after his own wore out, there in the middle of Five Mile Wood, poor frightened thing."

Mag, coming in with a towel, shook her head. "He looks nae frightened ta me, Master Robin. Just fierce. Like one of your birds."

The man smiled and held on to the boy while the two women clucked and clacked around the great tub. When at last they had emptied enough water and were satisfied with its temperature, Mag nodded and Master Robin dropped the boy in.

The boy had no fear of water, but it was not what he expected. It was hot. *Hot!* River water was always cold, and even in the lower pools—the ones he had dammed up for fishing—the water below the sun-warmed surface was always cold enough to make his ankles ache if he stayed in too long. He wanted to howl, but he would not give his captors the satisfaction. He wanted to leap out of the bath, but the Robin-man's great hand was still on him. Soon the fear and the warmth together quite paralyzed him. He had missed his afternoon nap tracking the man and he had missed his day's meager meals as well. Robin kept talking in that soft, steady voice.

The boy closed his eyes and surrendered to the warmth and to sleep and to a new dream.

In the new dream he was warm and safe and his stomach was altogether full. He was cradled in the wet and the warm. There was a humming sound, a rhythm that, he realized finally, was his own heart beating. The water and the warmth seemed to pulse with that same beat. And then from far away, there was a small pinprick of light, like the eyes of animals at night. The light came closer. And opened wider. He was forced to look at it—and it was the sun.

He was no longer in the water when he woke but in some kind of closed, warm room with a soft and wonderful smell. Untangling himself from the coverings, he looked around. The first part of the smell was like dry grass and he realized that was under him. But there was another smell coming from the floor. He peered over the edge of the mattress and saw that there was food.

He climbed off the bed and walked over to the food cautiously, checking first that neither the Robin-man nor Mag or Nell were around. But he was alone in the closed-in room.

Bending down, he breathed in the smell of the warm loaf. *Bread.* He spoke it. "Bread." He had loved it once, he remembered. Covered with something. A golden slab sat next to the loaf, and it had little smell but the color was as bright as a spring bird's feather. *Butter,* that was it. "But-ter." He said it aloud and loved the sound of it. "But-ter." He put his face close to the butter and stuck out his tongue, licking across the surface. Then he took the bread and tore off a piece and dragged it across the butter leaving a strange, deep gouge in the yellow slab. As he stuffed the piece in his mouth, he spoke aloud, "Bread and butter." The words were mangled in his full mouth, but he understood them with such a sharp insight that he was forced to shout them. The words along with the pieces of bread spat from his mouth. He laughed and scrambled to pick up the pieces and pushed them back in again.

Then he sat down, cross-legged by the tray, and tore off more hunks of bread, smearing it with so much butter that soon his hands and elbows and even his stomach bore testimony to his greed. At last he finished the bread and butter and licked the last crumbs from the tray and the floor around it.

There was a cup of hot water the color of leaf-mold on the tray as well, and he slurped it up, surprised that it, too, was warm. And sweet. He knew then that it was not water at all, but he could not recall its name.

"Names," he whispered to himself, and named again all the things that had been given back to him, starting with the bread: "bread, butter, horse, dog, hens, jerkin, coat." Then he added but not out loud, *Master Robin, Mag, and Nell.* He patted his greasy stomach and grunted happily. He could not remember ever being this warm and this full. Not ever.

He looked around the room slowly. There were two windows and the light shining through them reminded him of the light through the heavy interlacing of the trees in his forest. It fell to the floor in strange dusty patterns. Crawling over to the light, he tried to catch the motes in his hand, but each time he snatched at the dusty light, they disappeared and when he opened his hand, it was empty.

Standing, he looked at the window and the fields and forest beyond. Then he thrust his head forward and was painfully surprised by the glass. "Hard air," he said at first before his mind recalled the word to him: *window*. He had a sudden illumination, a dreamlike memory that assembled like colored glass shards in a pattern that formed bit by bit. Sometimes, he remembered and smiled at it, sometimes windows had many little pieces that made pictures. Of animals and people and grass and trees.

He tried to push open the glass, but he could not move it, so he left that window and tried the other. He went back and forth between them, pushing and leaving little marks on the glass. Angry then, he went to the door and shoved his shoulder against it. It would not open and he could not lift the latch.

So then he knew he was a prisoner in the room. The fields he could see through the glass and the tall familiar trees beyond were lost to him. He put his head back and howled. The long rise and fall of sound comforted him.

Then he went back to the bed and lay down beside it, pulling the covers onto the floor and making a nest of them. He slept.

When he woke again the room was darker and the light through the windows not so pure but shaded. There was a new loaf and a bowl of milk by the door. He stood and walked warily over to it. Then in a sudden fit of anger, he kicked the bowl over and screamed.

A few hours later, when the door remained shut against him and he had urinated all around the bed, hunger led him back to the loaf. He ate it savagely and sniffed around the place where the milk had spilled on the floor, but it had all soaked in.

Bored and angry, he paced back and forth between the window and the door, then he began to trot, and finally run around the room until he was out of breath. Standing in the middle of the room, he threw back his head to howl once again, but this time his howl died away in a series of short gasps and moans. He curled into the covers and wept, something he had not done in almost a year.

When the sounds of his weeping had stopped and he drifted into sleep the door into the room opened slowly. Master Robin entered and exchanged the empty bowl and tray for another, one with a bit of meat stew and milky porridge. Then he picked the boy up carefully and settled him into the bed. He stroked the boy's matted hair, brushing it from the wide forehead.

"There, there, my boy," he murmured in that soothing low voice. "First we'll tame you, then we'll name you. And then you'll claim your own."

The voice, the words, the warmth entered into the boy's dreams and, dreaming, he smiled and wiped his finger along his cheek. Then the finger found its way into his mouth.

The next dawn was the repeat of the first, and the next and the next. By the fifth day the room smelled and the floors bore the reminders of his filthy woods habits. But this time when the boy woke, Master Robin was there next to him, lying close and stroking his head.

"Come my boy, let me help you now, let me show you now."

The boy lowered his gaze, unable to quite meet the man's eyes, his skin quivering under the soft touch, the soft words.

The man rose from the bed and went over to the door where the tray full of food sat. This food was still warm and the smell seemed to overpower the musky, closed-in odor of the room.

Involuntarily, the boy licked his upper lip, then as if ashamed, wiped the back of his hand across his mouth. When Master Robin sat down on the bed with the tray, the boy reached over to grab the loaf. The man slapped his hand.

The sting did not hurt as much as the surprise. And then the memory of that other slap, when he was holding a joint of meat, jolted through him. "Forgive..." he said in a whisper, as if trying out a new tongue.

The man hugged him suddenly, fiercely. "There is nothing to forgive, young one. Just slow down. The bread will not run away. It is manners of the house and not the woods I am about to teach you."

The words meant less than the hug, of course. The boy sat back and waited.

Master Robin broke the bread into two sections. Then he picked up a silver stick with a rounded end and stuck it in the bowl of porridge. "Spoon," he said.

The boy whispered back, "Spoon." He put out his hand and his fingers closed around the handle of the spoon with a memory of their own. He ate the porridge greedily but with a measure of care as well, frequently stopping to check out Master Robin's reaction through the corners of his eyes.

"Good boy. Good. So you are no stranger to a spoon. How long were you in that woods, I wonder? Long enough, though. Long enough to go wild. Ah well, we'll tame you. I'm not a falconer for nought. I have a long patience with wild things. Eat then. Eat and rest. This afternoon, after we dress you, I'll take you out to the mews to see the hawks."

When the man left with the tray, the boy sat on the bed and watched. He made no attempt to follow out the door. There had been a promise. That much he had understood. A promise of a trip outside. It was enough.

However, he was too excited to nap again and he wandered around the room, not restlessly or angrily this time, but to catalog the room's contents. It was *his* room now. He had made it his, first by marking it and then by feeling safe in it. There was the bed and its rumpled covers, the rush-strewn floor, and a large closed wooden wardrobe he could not open. To one side of the bed was a small table that occasionally held a candle. He remembered its light when once he had awakened in the night. There was no candle there now. Instead a large bowl and jug stood there. He peered into both. They were empty.

He went to the window and looked out. A cow grazed on the open meadow, fastened by a chain to its spot. Near it two large brown dogs ran back and forth in some kind of frantic game for which only they seemed to understand the rules. The boy put his hand to the window and drew a line down the middle several inches long. ∫ He looked at it and then, ever so carefully, drew a line across the middle.

✝ After a moment of thought he drew a round thing on top. ⳨ Then he stopped and shook his head. The figure was incomplete. It needed something. He stood back from the window trying to puzzle it out, but the lines blurred together, then faded.

When he turned around, Master Robin was standing in the room and beside him were the two women.

"Hallo," said the man. "We've brought you some clothes."

The older woman wrinkled her nose as she looked around the room. The younger one gave a tentative smile. Then all three moved toward the boy who waited stone still.

It took them quite a while to dress him, for he had forgotten what to do and was uncomfortable with so many hands on him. And once he snarled and the women drew back. But Master Robin persevered and, at last, the boy had on short trews, a shirt, and a vest, which were the names Mag gave the clothes. And he wore as well a peculiar harness of plaited rope that went around each shoulder and across his chest and back, with a lead that Master Robin kept tight in his hand. It reminded the boy of the chain that held the cow but he did not try to pull it away. It made him feel part of the man, and he liked that now.

Then Master Robin sent the two women from the room, and they scuttled like badgers running back to the sett. The boy laughed as they closed the door behind them, and that made Master Robin laugh, too.

"So, you can laugh and you can cry and you can speak some, too. You are no idiot, for all that Mag would have you so," said the soft voice. "Would you like to see the birds?"

His answer was to stand.

"Well. And well." Master Robin stood slowly and patted him, almost carelessly, on the head. "Tomorrow we will do somewhat with that hair."

He knocked on the door and there was a series of small sounds as the door was unlocked from the outside. Then they went from the safety of the room, the rope loose between them.

The birds were housed in a long low building, with horn in the small windows.

"The mews," Master Robin said as they entered. And he gave names to many things as they walked through the long room. "Door, perch, bird, lamp, rafters." And mimicking his tone, the boy repeated each with a kind of greed. In fact, his face looked as it had when he had smelled the first loaf of bread, his eyes squinting, chin up, a kind of feral anticipation.

They walked slowly through the sawdust on the floor, and the boy took it all as if it were both his very first and also his hundredth time in such a place.

At last they were before a trio of hooded birds on individual stands where the heavy sacking screens hanging from the perches moved slowly in the bit of wind like castle banners. Master Robin stood for a moment, nodding his head at the birds, hands behind his back. The boy echoed his stance.

Then, as if he could contain his excitement no longer, the boy turned to the man and whispered, "Bird. Hawk. Yours?" His voice was husky, deeper than most boys' his age.

The man was careful not to move but smiled slowly. "Aye," he said. "They are mine. They are mine because they have given some part of themselves to me. But not all of it. And not forever. I would not want them to give me all. And every day I must earn their trust again. With wild things there is no such word as *forever*."

The boy listened intently.

"I stood three nights running with the gos—there," said the man, nodding his head toward the bird furthest to the left. "He was on my fist the whole time."

"And tied?" the boy asked.

"Aye."

The boy nodded as if this had been a wise thing to do.

"When he bated, I put him back on my fist. Again and again. But gently. Firmly. And I sang to him. I spoke words to him all night."

"My hinny, my jo," the boy said in a passable imitation of the man.

"Aye. And stroked his talons with a feather and gave him meat. And after three days and nights without sleep, he allowed himself to nap on my fist. He gave himself to me in his sleep."

"In his sleep." The boy's voice was so soft that the man had to strain to hear it.

"The peregrine there," Master Robin said, indicating the middle bird, "is my oldest bird. She's a lovely one. An eyas."

"Eyas?"

"That means I took her from the nest myself. Nearly lost an eye doing it. There was another in the nest, but . . ." He stopped, aware that the boy was no longer listening.

The boy had moved forward several short steps until the rope had stretched between them. Standing just under the third bird's feet, he was staring up at it.

"Ah, that one, he's a *passager*, wild caught but not yet mature."

The hawk stirred as if it knew it was being talked about, and the bell on its jess rang out.

At the sound the boy jumped back. Then he strained forward again against the rope.

"You like my merlin best, then?" Master Robin asked in his low voice.

The boy turned sharply and stared at him wide-eyed. His mouth dropped open and he put his hands out as if he had suddenly turned blind.

Robin gathered the child into his arms. "What is it then? What is it, wild one? What did I say? What have I done?"

The boy tore from him and stared again at the hooded bird who, unaccountably, began to rock back and forth from one foot to another, its bell jangling madly. "Name," the boy said and rocked back and forth with the bird. "Name."

The man stared at the boy and the bird, first only his eyes moving, then his head. With a final shock of recognition, he turned, plunged his hand into the nearby water barrel, and then reached for the boy. With his finger, he drew a cross on the boy's forehead, one swift line down, a second across, under the tangle of elfknots in his hair.

"I see," he said. "I understand. You are as small and as fierce and as independent as my *passager*. And for some reason his name is yours. So I baptize you Merlin. In the

name of the Father and of the Son and of the Holy Spirit."
So saying, he jerked the knife from his belt and cut the
harness off the boy.

For a moment the boy stared up into the man's eyes
directly. Then he smiled and held out his hand for memory,
at last, had come flooding through him when he was given
back his name.

"Lord," said he, "summon to you Myrddin the bard
of Gwythheyrn, for he knows how to conceive strange
things by his unfailing immortal artistry."

—Historia Regum Britanniae
by Geoffrey of Monmouth

Dream Reader

Once upon a time—which is how stories about magic and wizardry are supposed to begin—on a fall morning a boy stood longingly in front of a barrow piled high with apples. It was in the town of Gwethern, the day of the market fair.

The boy was almost a man and he did not complain about his empty stomach. His back still hurt from the flogging he had received just a week past, but he did not complain about that either. He had been beaten and sent away for lying. He was always being sent away from place to place for lying. The problem was, he never lied. He simply saw truth differently from other folk. On the slant.

His name was Merrillin but he called himself Hawk, another kind of lie because he was nothing at all like a hawk, being cowering and small from his many beatings and lack of steady food. Still he dreamed of becoming a hawk, fiercely independent and no man's prey, and the naming was his first small step toward what seemed an unobtainable goal.

But that was the other thing about Merrillin the Hawk. Not only did he see the truth slantwise, but he dreamed. And his dreams, in strange, uncounted ways, seemed to come true.

So Merrillin stood in front of the barrow on a late fall day and told himself a lie; that the apple would fall into his hand of its own accord as if the barrow were a tree letting loose its fruit. He even reached over and touched the apple he wanted, a rosy round one that promised to be full of sweet juices and crisp meat. And just in case, he touched a second apple as well, one that was slightly wormy and a bit yellow with age.

"You boy," came a shout from behind the barrow, and a face as yellow and sunken as the second apple, with veins as large as worm runnels across the nose, popped into view.

Merrillin stepped back, startled.

A stick came down on his hand, sharp and painful as a firebrand. "If you do not mean to buy, you cannot touch."

"How do you know he does not mean to buy?" asked a voice from behind Merrillin.

It took all his concentration not to turn. He feared the man behind him might have a stick as well, though his voice seemed devoid of the kind of anger that always preceded a beating.

"A rag of cloth hung on bones, that's all he is," said the cart man, wiping a dirty rag across his mouth. "No one in Gwethern has seen him before. He's no mother's son, by the dirt on him. So where would such a one find coins to pay, cheeky beggar?"

There was a short bark of laughter from the man behind. "Cheeky beggar is it?"

Merrillin dared a glance at the shadow the man cast at his feet. The shadow was cloaked. That was a good sign, for he would be a stranger to Gwethern. No one here affected such dress. Courage flooded through him and he almost turned around when the man's hand touched his mouth.

"You are right, he is a cheeky beggar. And that is where he keeps his coin—in his cheek." The cloaked man laughed again, the same sharp, yipping sound, drawing an appreciative echo from the crowd that was just starting to gather. Entertainment was rare in Gwethern. "Open your mouth, boy, and give the man his coin."

Merrillin was so surprised, his mouth dropped open on its own, and a coin fell from his lips into the cloaked man's hand.

"Here," the man said, his hand now on Merrillin's shoulder. He flipped the coin into the air, it turned twice over before the cart man grabbed it out of the air, bit it, grunted, and shoved it into his purse.

The cloaked man's hand left Merrillin's shoulder and picked up the yellowing apple, dropping it neatly into Merrillin's hand. Then his voice whispered into the boy's ear. "If you wish to repay me, look for the green wagon, the castle on wheels."

When Merrillin turned to stutter out his thanks, the man had vanished into the crowd. That was just as well, though, since it was hardly thanks Merrillin was thinking of. Rather he wanted to tell the cloaked man that he had done only what was expected and that another lie had come true for Merrillin, on the slant.

After eating every bit of the apple, his first meal in two days, and setting the little green worm that had been in it on a stone, Merrillin looked for the wagon. It was not hard to find.

Parked under a chestnut tree whose leaves were spotted with brown and gold, the wagon was as green as Mab's gown, as green as the first early shoots of spring. It was indeed a castle on wheels, for the top of the wagon was vaulted over. There were three windows, four walls, and a door as well. Two docile drab-colored mules were hitched to it and were nibbling on the few brown blades of grass beneath the tree. Along the wagon's sides was writing, but as Merrillin could not read, he could only guess at it. There were pictures, too: a tall, amber-eyed mage with a conical hat was dancing across a starry night, a dark-haired princess in rainbow robes played on a harp with thirteen strings. Merrillin could not read—but he could count. He walked toward the wagon.

"So, boy, have you come to pay what you owe?" asked a soft voice, followed by the trill of a mistle thrush.

At first Merrillin could not see who was speaking, but then something moved at one of the windows, a pale moon of a face. It was right where the face of the painted princess should have been. Until it moved, Merrillin had thought it part of the painting. With a bang, the window was slammed shut and then he saw the painted face on the glass. It resembled the other face only slightly.

A woman stepped through the door and stared at him. He thought her the most beautiful person he had ever seen. Her long dark hair was unbound and fell to her waist. She wore a dress of scarlet wool and jewels in her ears. A yellow purse hung from a braided belt and jangled as she moved, as if it were covered with tiny bells. As he watched, she bound up her hair with a single swift motion into a net of scarlet linen.

She smiled. "Ding-dang-dong, cat's got your tongue, then?"

When he didn't answer, she laughed and sat down on the top step of the wagon. Then she reached back behind her and pulled out a harp exactly like the one painted on the wagon's side. Strumming, she began to sing:

> *"A boy with eyes a somber blue*
> *Will never ever come to rue,*
> *A boy with..."*

"Are you singing about me?" asked Merrillin.

"Do you think I am singing about you?" the woman asked and then hummed another line.

"If not now, you will some day," Merrillin said.

"I believe you," said the woman, but she was busy tuning her harp at the same time. It was as if Merrillin did not really exist for her except as an audience.

"Most people do not," Merrillin said, walking over. He put his hand on the top step, next to her bare foot. "Believe me, I mean. But I never tell lies."

She looked up at that and stared at him as if really seeing him for the first time. "People who never tell lies are a wonder. All people lie sometime." She strummed a discordant chord.

Merrillin looked at the ground. "I am not *all people*."

She began picking a quick, bright tune, singing:

> "If you never ever lie
> You are a better soul than I..."

Then she stood and held up the harp behind her. It disappeared into the wagon. "But you did not answer my question, boy."

"What question?"

"Have you come to pay what you owe?"

Puzzled Merrillin said: "I did not answer because I did not know you were talking to me. I owe nothing to you."

"Ah, but you owe it me," came a lower voice from inside the wagon where it was dark. A man emerged and even though he was not wearing the cloak, Merrillin knew him at once. The voice was the same, gentle and ironic. He was the mage on the wagon's side; the slate gray hair was the same—and the amber eyes.

"I do not owe you either, sir."

"What of the apple, boy?"

Merrillin started to cringe, thought better of it, and looked straightaway into the man's eyes. "The apple was *meant* to come to me, sir."

"Then why came you to the wagon?" asked the woman, smoothing her hands across the red dress. "If not to pay."

"As the apple was meant to come into my hands, so I was meant to come into yours."

The woman laughed. "Only you hoped the mage would not eat you up and put your little green worm on a rock for some passing scavenger."

Merrillin's mouth dropped open. "How did you know?"

"Bards *know* everything," she said.

"And *tell* everything as well," said the mage. He clapped her on the shoulder and she went, laughing, through the door.

Merrillin nodded to himself. "It was the window," he whispered.

"Of course it was the window," said the mage. "And if you wish to talk to yourself, make it *sotto voce*, under the breath. A whisper is no guarantee of secrets."

"Sotto voce," Merrillin said.

"The soldiers brought the phrase, but it rides the market roads now," said the mage.

"Sotto voce," Merrillin said again, punctuating his memory.

"I like you, boy," said the mage. "I collect oddities."

"Did you collect the bard, sir?"

Looking quickly over his shoulder, the mage said, "Her?"

"Yes, sir."

"I did."

"How is she an oddity?" asked Merrillin. "I think she is—" he took a gulp, "—wonderful."

"That she is; quite, quite wonderful, my Viviane, and she well knows it," the mage replied. "She has a range of four octaves and can mimic any bird or beast I name." He paused. "And a few I cannot."

"Viviane," whispered Merrillin. Then he said the name without making a sound.

The mage laughed heartily. "You are an oddity, too, boy. I thought so at the first when you walked into the market fair with nothing to sell and no purse with which to buy. I asked, and no one knew you. Yet you stood in front of the barrow as if you owned the apples. When the stick fell, you did not protest; when the coin dropped from your lips, you said not a word. But I could feel your anger and surprise and—something more. You are an oddity. I sniffed it out with my nose from the first and my nose—" he tapped it with his forefinger, managing to look both wise and ominous at once "—my nose, like you, never lies. Do you think yourself odd?"

Merrillin closed his eyes for a moment, a gesture the mage would come to know well. When he opened them again, his eyes were no longer the somber blue that Viviane had sung about but were the blue of a bleached out winter sky. "I have dreams," he said.

The mage held his breath, his wisdom being as often in silence as in words.

"I dreamed of a wizard and a woman who lived in a castle green as early spring grass. Hawks flew about the turrets and a bear squatted on the throne. I do not know what it all means, but now that I have seen the green wagon, I am sure you are the wizard and the woman, Viviane."

"Do you dream often?" asked the mage, slowly coming down the steps of the wagon and sitting on the lowest stair.

Merrillin nodded.

"And do your dreams often come true?" he asked. Then he added, quickly, "No, you do not have to answer that."

Merrillin nodded again.

"Always?"

Merrillin closed his eyes, then opened them.

"Tell me," said the mage.

"I dare not. When I tell, I am called a liar or hit. Or both. I do not think I want to be hit anymore."

The mage laughed again, this time with his head back. When he finished, he narrowed his eyes and looked at the boy. "I have never hit anyone in my life. And telling lies is an essential part of magic. You lie with your hands like this." And so saying, he reached behind Merrillin's ear and pulled out a bouquet of meadowsweet, wintergreen, and a single blue aster. "You see, my hands told the lie that flowers grow in the dirt behind your ear. And your eyes took it in."

Merrillin laughed, a funny crackling sound, as if he were not much used to laughter.

"But do not let Viviane know you tell lies," said the mage, leaning forward and whispering. "She is as practiced in her anger as she is on the harp. I may never swot a liar, but she is the very devil when her temper's aroused."

"I will not," said Merrillin solemnly. They shook hands on it, only when Merrillin drew away his grasp, he had a small copper coin in his palm.

"Buy yourself a meat pie, boy," said the mage. "And then come along with us. I think you will be a very fine addition to our collection."

"Thank you, sir," gasped Merrillin.

"Not *sir*. My name is Ambrosius, because of my amber eyes. Did you notice them? Ambrosius the Wandering Mage. And what is your name? I cannot keep calling you 'boy.'"

"My name is Merrillin but . . ." he hesitated and looked down.

"I will not hit you and you may keep the coin whatever you say," Ambrosius said.

"But I would like to be called Hawk."

"Hawk, is it?" The mage laughed again. "Perhaps you will grow into that name, but it seems to me that you are mighty small and a bit thin for a hawk."

A strange sharp cackling sound came from the interior of the wagon, a high *ki-ki-ki-ki*.

The mage looked in and back. "Viviane says you *are* a hawk, but a small one — the merlin. And that is, quite happily, close to your Christian name as well. Will it suit?"

"Merlin," whispered Merrillin, his hand clutched tightly around the coin. Then he looked up, his eyes gone the blue of the aster. "That was the hawk in my dream, Ambrosius. That was the sound he made. A merlin. It has to be my true name."

"Good. Then it is settled," said the mage standing. "Fly off to your pie, Hawk Merlin, and then fly quickly back to me. We go tomorrow to Carmarthen. There's to be a great holy day fair. Viviane will sing. I will do my magic. And you — well, we shall have to figure out what you can do. But it will be something quite worthy, I am sure. I tell you, young Merlin, there are fortunes to be made on the road if you can sing in four voices and pluck flowers out of the air."

The road was a gentle winding path through valleys and alongside streams. The trees were still gold in most places, but on the far ridges the forests were already bare.

As the wagon bounced along, Viviane sang songs about Robin of the Wood in a high, sweet voice and the Battle of the Trees in a voice deep as thunder. And in a middle voice she sang a lusty ballad about a bold warrior that made Merlin's cheeks turn pink and hot.

Ambrosius shortened the journey with his wonder tales.

And as he talked, he made coins walk across his knuckles
and found two quail's eggs behind Viviane's left ear. Once
he pulled a turtledove out of Merlin's shirt, which surprised
the dove more than the boy. The bird flew off onto a low
branch of an ash tree and plucked its breast feathers furiously
until the wagon had passed by.

They were two days traveling and one day resting by a
lovely bright pond rimmed with willows.

"Carmarthen is over that small hill," pointed out the
mage. "But it will wait on us. The fair does not begin until
tomorrow. Besides, we have fishing to do. And a man—
whether mage or murderer—always can find time to fish!"
He took Merlin down to the pond where he quickly proved
himself a bad angler but a merry companion, telling fish
stories late into the night. All he caught was a turtle. It was
Merlin who pulled up the one small spotted trout they roasted
over the fire that night and shared three ways.

Theirs was not the only wagon on the road before dawn,
but it was the gaudiest by far. Peddlers' children leaped off
their own wagons to run alongside and beg the magician
for a trick. He did one for each child and asked for no coins
at all, even though Viviane chided him.

"Do not scold, Viviane. Each child will bring another to
our wagon once we are in the town. They will be our best
criers," Ambrosius said, as he made a periwinkle appear
from under the chin of a dirty-faced tinker lass. She giggled
and ran off with the flower.

At first each trick made Merlin gasp with delight. But
partway through the trip, he began to notice from where the
flowers and coins and scarves and eggs really appeared—
out of the vast sleeves of the mage's robe. He started watching Ambrosius' hands carefully through slotted eyes, and
unconsciously his own hands began to imitate them.

Viviane reached over and, holding the reins with one
hand, slapped his fingers so hard they burned. "Do not do
that. It is bad enough he does the tricks for free on the road,
but you would beggar us for sure if you give them away
forever. Idiot!"

After the scolding, Merlin sat sullenly inside the dark-
ened wagon practicing his sotto voce with curses he had

heard but had never dared repeat aloud. Embarrassment rather than anger sent a kind of ague to his limbs. Eventually, though, he wore himself out and fell asleep. He dreamed a wicked little dream about Viviane, in which a whitethorn tree fell upon her. When he woke, he was ashamed of the dream and afraid of it as well, but he did not know how to change it. His only comfort was that his dreams did not come true literally. *On the slant,* he reminded himself, which lent him small comfort.

He was still puzzling this out when the mules slowed and he became aware of a growing noise. Moving to the window, he stared out past the painted face.

If Gwethern had been a bustling little market town, Carmarthen had to be the very center of the commercial world. Merlin saw gardens and orchards outside the towering city walls though he also noted that the gardens were laid out in a strange pattern and some of the trees along the northern edges were ruined and the ground around them was raw and wounded. There were many spotty pastures where sheep and kine grazed on the late fall stubble. The city walls were made up of large blocks of limestone. How anyone could have moved such giant stones was a mystery to him. Above the walls he could glimpse crenellated towers from which red and white banners waved gaudily in the shifting fall winds, first north, then west.

Merlin could contain himself no longer and scrambled through the wagon door, squeezing in between Ambrosius and Viviane.

"Look, oh look!" he cried.

Viviane smiled at the childish outburst, but the mage touched his hand.

"It is not enough just to look, Merlin. You must look—and remember."

"Remember—what?" asked Merlin.

"The eyes and ears are different listeners," said the mage. "But both feed into magecraft. Listen. What do you hear?"

Merlin strained, tried to sort out the many sounds, and said at last, "It is very noisy."

Viviane laughed. *"I* hear carts growling along, and voices, many different tongues. A bit of Norman, some Saxon, Welsh, and Frankish. There is a hawk screaming in the sky behind us. And a loud, heavy clatter coming from behind the walls. Something being built, I would guess."

Merlin listened again. He could hear the carts and voices easily. The hawk was either silent now or beyond his ken. But because she mentioned it, he could hear the heavy rhythmic pounding of building like a bass note, grounding the entire song of Carmarthen. "Yes," he said, with a final exhalation.

"And what do you see?" asked Ambrosius.

Determined to match Viviane's ears with his eyes, Merlin began a litany of wagons and wagoners, beasts straining to pull, and birds restrained in cages. He described jongleurs and farmers and weavers and all their wares. As they passed through the gates of the city and under the portcullis, he described it as well.

"Good," said Ambrosius. "And what of those soldiers over there." He nodded his head slightly to the left.

Merlin turned to stare at them.

"No, never look directly on soldiers, highwaymen, or kings. Look through the slant of your eyes," whispered Viviane, reining in the mules.

Merlin did as she instructed, delighted to be once more in her good graces. "There are ten of them," he said.

"And what do they wear?" prompted Ambrosius.

"Why, their uniforms. And helms."

"What color helms?" Viviane asked.

"Silver, as helms are wont. But six have red plumes, four white." Then as an afterthought, he added, "And they all carry swords."

"The swords are not important," said Ambrosius, "but note the helms. Ask yourself why some should be sporting red plumes, some white. Ask yourself if these are two different armies of two different lords. And if so, why are they both here?"

"I do not know," answered Merlin. "Why?"

Ambrosius laughed. "I do not know either. Yet. But it is something odd to be tucked away. And remember—I collect oddities."

Viviane clicked to the mules with her tongue and slapped their backs with the reins. They started forward again.

"Once around the square, Viviane, then we will choose

our spot. Things are already well begun," said the mage. "There are a juggler and a pair of acrobats and several strolling players, though none—I wager—with anything near your range. But I see no other masters of magic. We shall do well here."

In a suit of green and gold—the gold a cotte of the mage's that Viviane had tailored to fit him, the green his old hose sewn over with gold patches and bells—Merlin strode through the crowd with a tambourine. It was his job to collect the coins after each performance. On the first day folk were liable to be the most generous, afterward husbanding their coins for the final hours of the fair, at least that was what Viviane had told him. Still he was surprised by the waterfall of copper pennies that cascaded into his tambourine.

"Our boy Merlin will pass amongst you, a small hawk in the pigeons," Ambrosius had announced before completing his final trick, the one in which Viviane was shut up in a box and subsequently disappeared into the wagon.

Merlin had glowed at the name pronounced so casually aloud, and at the claim of possession. *Our* boy, Ambrosius had said. Merlin repeated the phrase sotte voce to himself and smiled. The infectious smile brought even more coins, though he was unaware of it.

It was after their evening performance when Viviane had sung in three different voices, including a love song about a shepherd and the ewe lamb that turned into a lovely maiden who fled from him over a cliff, that a broad-faced soldier with a red plume in his helm parted the teary-eyed crowd. Coming up to the wagon stage, he announced, "The Lady Renwein would have you come tomorrow evening to the old palace and sends this as way of a promise. There will be more after a satisfactory performance. It is in honor of her upcoming wedding." He dropped a purse into Ambrosius' hand.

The mage bowed low and then, with a wink, began drawing a series of colored scarves from behind the soldier's ear. They were all shades of red: crimson, pink, vermilion, flame, scarlet, carmine, and rose.

"For your lady," Ambrosius said, holding out the scarves.

The soldier laughed aloud and took them. "The lady's colors. She will be pleased. Though not, I think, his lordship."

"The white soldiers, then, are his?" asked Ambrosius.

Ignoring the question, the soldier said, "Be in the kitchen by nones. We ring the bells here. The duke is most particular."

"Is dinner included?" asked Viviane.

"Yes, mistress," the soldier replied. "You shall eat what the cook eats." He turned and left.

"Then let us hope," said Viviane to his retreating back, "that we like what the cook likes."

Merlin dreamed that night and woke screaming but could not recall exactly what he had dreamed. The mage's hand was on his brow and Viviane wrung out cool water onto a cloth for him.

"Too much excitement for one day," she said, making a clucking sound with her tongue.

"And too many meat pies," added the mage, nodding.

The morning of the second day of the holy day fair came much too soon. And noisily. When Merlin went to don his green-and-gold suit, Ambrosius stayed him.

"Save that for the lady's performance. I need you in your old cotte to go around the fair. And remember—use your ears and eyes."

Nodding, Merlin scrambled into his old clothes. They had been tidied up by Viviane, but he was aware, for the first time, of how really shabby and threadbare they were. Ambrosius slipped him a coin.

"You earned this. Spend it as you will. But not on food, boy. We will feast enough at the duke's expense."

Clutching the coin, Merlin escaped into the early morning crowds. In his old clothes, he was unremarked, just another poor lad eyeing the wonders at the holy day fair.

At first he was seduced by the stalls. The variety of foods and cloth and toys and entertainments were beyond anything he had ever imagined. But halfway around the second time, he remembered his charge. *Eyes and ears*. He did not know exactly what Ambrosius would find useful but he was determined to uncover something.

* * *

"It was between the Meadowlands Jugglers and a stall of spinach pies," he told Ambrosius later, wrinkling his nose at the thought of spinach baked in a flakey crust. "A white plumed soldier and a red were quarreling. It began with name calling. Red called white, 'Dirty men of a dirty duke,' and white countered with 'Spittle of the Lady Cock.' And they would have fallen to, but a ball from the jugglers landed at their feet and the crowd surged over to collect it."

"So there is no love lost between the two armies," mused Ambrosius. "I wonder if they were the cause of the twisted earth around the city walls."

"And after that I watched carefully for pairs of soldiers. They were everywhere matched, one red and one white. And the names between them bounced back and forth like an apple between boys."

The mage pulled on his beard thoughtfully. "What other names did you hear?"

"She was called Dragonlady, Lady Death, and the Open Way."

Ambrosius laughed. "Colorful. And one must wonder how accurate."

"And the duke was called Pieless, the Ewe's Own Lover, and Draco," said Merlin, warming to his task.

"Scurrilous and the Lord knows how well-founded. But two dragons quarreling in a single nest? It will make an unsettling performance at best. One can only wonder why two such creatures decided to wed." Ambrosius worked a coin across his knuckles, back and forth, back and forth. It was a sign he was thinking.

"Surely, for love?" whispered Merlin.

Viviane, who had been sitting quietly, darning a colorful petticoat, laughed. "Princes never marry for love, little hawk. For money, for lands, for power—yes. Love they find elsewhere or not at all. That is why I would never be a prince."

Ambrosius seemed not to hear her, but Merlin took in every word and savored the promise he thought he heard.

They arrived at the old castle as the bells chimed nones. And the castle was indeed old; its keep from the days of the Romans was mottled and pocked but was still the most solid part of the building. Even Merlin, unused as he was to the ways of builders, could see that the rest was of shoddy material and worse workmanship.

"The sounds of building we heard from far off must be a brand-new manor being constructed," said Ambrosius. "For the new-wedded pair."

And indeed the cook, whose taste in supper clearly matched Viviane's, agreed. "The duke's father fair beggared our province fighting off imagined invaders, and his son seems bent on finishing the job. He even invited the bloody-minded Saxons in to help." He held up his right hand and made the sign of horns and spat through it. "Once, though you'd hardly credit it, this was a countryside of lucid fountains and transparent rivers. Now it's often dry as dust, though it was one of the prettiest places in all Britain. And if the countryside is in tatters, the duke's coffers are worse. That is why he has made up his mind to marry the Lady Renwein. She has as much money as she has had lovers, so they say, and that is not the British way. But the duke is besotted with both her counte and her coinage. And even I must admit she has made a difference. Why, they are building a new great house upon the site of the old Roman barracks. The duke is having it constructed on the promise of her goods."

Viviane made no comment but kept eating. Ambrosius, who always ate sparingly before a performance, listened intently, urging the cook on with well-placed questions. Following Viviane's actions, Merlin stuffed himself and almost made himself sick again. He curled up in a corner near the hearth to sleep. The last thing he heard was the cook's continuing complaint.

"I know not when we shall move into the new house. I long for the larger hearth promised, for now with the red guards to feed as well as the duke's white—*and* the Saxon retainers—I need more. But the building goes poorly."

"Is that so?" interjected Ambrosius.

"Aye. The foundation does not hold. What is built up by day falls down by night. There is talk of witchcraft."

"Is there?" Ambrosius asked smoothly.

"Aye, the Saxons claim it against us. British witches, they cry. And they want blood to cleanse it."

"Do they?"

A hand on his shoulder roused Merlin, but he was still partially within the vivid dream.

"The dragons . . ." he murmured and opened his eyes.

"Hush," came Ambrosius' voice. "Hush—and remember. You called out many times in your sleep: dragons and castles, water and blood, but what it all means you kept to yourself. So remember the dream, all of it. And I will tell you when to spin out the tale to catch the conscience of Carmarthen in its web. If I am right . . ." He touched his nose.

Merlin closed his eyes again and nodded. He did not open them again until Viviane began fussing with his hair, running a comb through the worst tangles and pulling at his cotte. She tied a lover's knot of red and white ribbands around his sleeve, then moved back.

"Open your eyes, boy. You are a sight." She laughed and pinched one cheek.

The touch of her hand made his cheeks burn. He opened his eyes and saw the kitchen abustle with servants. The cook, now too busy to chat with them further, was working at the hearth, basting and stirring and calling out a string of instructions to his overworked crew. "Here, Stephen, more juice. Wine up to the tables and hurry, Mag—they are pounding their feet upon the floor. The soup is hot enough, the tureens must be run up, and mind the handles. Use a cloth, Nan, stupid girl. And where are the sharp knives? These be dull as Saxon wit. Come, Stephen, step lively; the pies must come out the oast or they burn. Now!"

Merlin wondered that he could keep it all straight.

The while Ambrosius in one corner limbered up his fingers, having already checked out his apparatus and Viviane, sitting down at the table, began to tune her harp. Holding it on her lap, her head cocked to one side, she sang a note then tuned each string to it. It was a wonder she could hear in all that noise—the cook shouting, Stephen clumping around and bumping into things, Nan whining, and Mag cursing back at the cook—but she did not seem to mind, her face drawn up with passionate intensity.

Into the busyness strode a soldier. When he came up to the hearth, Merlin could see it was the same one who had first tendered them the invitation to perform. His broad, homey face was split by a smile, wine and plenty of hot food having worked their own magic.

"Come, mage. And you, singer. We are ready when you are."

Ambrosius gestured to three large boxes. "Will you lend a hand?"

The soldier grunted.

"And my boy comes, too," said Ambrosius.

Putting his head to one side as if considering, the soldier asked, "Is he strong enough to carry these? He looks small and puling."

"He can carry if he has to, but he is more than that to us."

The soldier laughed. "You will have no need of a tambourine boy to pass among the gentlefolk and soldiers. Her ladyship will see that you are well enough paid."

Ambrosius stood very tall and dropped his voice to a deep, harsh whisper. "I have performed in higher courts than this. I know what is fit for fairs and what is fit for a great hall. You know not to whom you speak."

The soldier drew back.

Viviane smiled but carefully, so that the soldier could not see it, and played three low notes on the harp.

Merlin did not move. It was as if for a moment the entire kitchen had turned to stone.

Then the soldier gave a short, barking laugh, but his face was wary. "Do not mock me, mage. I saw him do nothing but pick up coins."

"That is because he only proffers his gifts for people of station. I am but a mage, a man of small magics and tricks that fool the eye. But the boy is something more." He walked toward Merlin slowly, his hand outstretched.

Still Merlin did not move, though imperceptibly he stood taller. Ambrosius put his hand on Merlin's shoulders.

"The boy is a reader of dreams," said the mage. "What he dreams comes true."

"Is this so?" asked the soldier, looking around.

"It is so," said Viviane.

Merlin closed his eyes for a moment, and when he opened them, they were the color of an ocean swell, blue-green washed with gray. "It is so," he said at last.

From the hearth where he was basting the joints of meat, the cook called out, "It is true that the boy dreamed here today. About two dragons. I heard him cry out in his sleep."

The soldier, who had hopes of a captaincy, thought a moment, then said, "Very well, all three of you come with me. Up the stairs. Now." He cornered young Stephen to carry the mage's boxes, and marched smartly out the door.

The others followed quickly, though Merlin hung back long enough to give the other boy a hand.

Viviane sang first, a medley of love songs that favored the duke and his lady in turn. With the skill of a seasoned entertainer, she inserted the Lady Renwein's name into her rhyme, but called the duke in the songs merely "The Duke of Carmarthen town." (Later she explained to Merlin that the only rhymes she had for the duke's name were either scurrilous or treasonous, and sang a couple of verses to prove it.) Such was her ability, each took the songs as flattering, though Merlin thought he detected a nasty undertone in them that made him uncomfortable. But Viviane was roundly applauded and at the end of her songs, two young soldiers picked her up between them and set her upon their table for an encore. She smiled prettily at them, but Merlin knew she hated their touch, for the smile was one she reserved for particularly messy children, drunken old men—and swine.

Deftly beginning his own performance at the moment Viviane ended hers, Ambrosius was able to cover any unpleasantness that might occur if one of the soldiers dared take liberties with Viviane as she climbed down from the tabletop. He began with silly tricks—eggs, baskets, even a turtle was plucked from the air or from behind an unsuspecting soldier's ear. The tortoise was the one the mage had found when they had been fishing.

Then Ambrosius moved on to finer tricks, guessing the name of a soldier's sweetheart, finding the red queen in a deck of cards missing yet discovering it under the Lady Renwein's plate, and finally making Viviane disappear and reappear in a series of boxes through which he had the soldiers thrust their swords.

The last trick brought great consternation to the guards, especially when blood appeared to leak from the boxes, blood which when examined later proved to be juices from the meat which Viviane had kept in a flask. And when she reappeared, whole, unharmed, and smiling once the swords had been withdrawn from the box, the great hall resounded with huzzahs.

The duke smiled and whispered to the Lady Renwein. She covered his hand with hers. When he withdrew his hand, the duke held out a plump purse. He jangled it loudly.

"We are pleased to offer you this, Ambrosius."

"Thank you, my lord. But we are not done yet," said the mage with a bow which, had it been a little less florid, would have been an insult. "I would introduce you to Merlin, our dream reader, who will tell you of a singular dream he had this day in your house."

Merlin came to the center of the room. He could feel his legs trembling. Ambrosius walked over to him and, turning his back to the duke, whispered to the boy. "Do not be afraid. Tell the dream and I will say what it means."

"Will you know?" asked Merlin.

"My eyes and ears know what needs be said here," said Ambrosius, "whatever the dream. You must trust me."

Merlin nodded and Ambrosius moved aside. The boy stood with his eyes closed and began to speak.

"I dreamed a tower of snow that in the day reached high up into the sky but at night melted to the ground. And there was much weeping and wailing in the country because the tower would not stand."

"The castle!" the duke gasped, but Lady Renwein placed her hand gently on his mouth.

"Hush, my lord," she whispered urgently. "Listen. Do not speak yet. This may be merely a magician's trick. After all, they have been in Carmarthen for two days already and surely there is talk of the building in the town."

Merlin, his eyes still closed, seemed not to hear them, but continued. "And then one man arose, a mage, who advised that the tower of icy water be drained in the morning instead of building atop it. It was done as he wished, though the soldiers complained bitterly of it. But at last the pool was drained and lo! there in the mud lay two great hollow stones as round and speckled and veined as gray eggs.

"Then the mage drew a sword and struck open the eggs. In the one was a dragon the color of wine, its eyes faceted as jewels. In the other a dragon the color of maggots, with eyes as tarnished as old coins.

"And when the two dragons saw that they were revealed, they turned not on the soldiers nor the mage but upon one another. At first the white dragon had the best of it and pushed the red to the very edge of the dry pool, but it so blooded its opponent that a new pool was formed, the color of the ocean beyond the waves. But then the red rallied and pushed the white back, and it slipped into the bloody pool and disappeared, never to be seen again whole.

"And the man who advised began to speak once more, but I awoke."

At that, Merlin opened his eyes and they were the blue of speedwells on a summer morn.

The Lady Renwein's face was dark and disturbed. In a low voice she said, "Mage, ask him what the dream means."

Ambrosius bowed very low this time, for he saw that while the duke might be easily cozzened, the Lady Renwein was no fool. When he stood straight again, he said, "The boy dreams, my lady, but he leaves it to me to make sense of what he dreams. Just as did his dear, dead mother before him."

Merlin, startled, looked at Viviane. She rolled her eyes up to stare at the broad beams of the ceiling and held her mouth still.

"His mother was a dream reader, too?" asked the duke.

"She was, though being a woman, dreamed of more homey things: the names of babes and whether they be boys or girls, and when to plant, and so forth."

The Lady Renwein leaned forward. "Then say, mage, what this dream of towers and dragons means."

"I will, my lady. It is not unknown to us that you have a house that will not stand. However, what young Merlin has dreamed is the reason for this. The house or tower of snow sinks every day into the ground; in the image of the dream, it melts. That is because there is a pool beneath it. Most likely the Romans built the conduits for their baths there. With the construction, there has been a leakage underground. The natural outflow has been damaged further by armies fighting. And so there has been a pooling under the foundation. Open up the work, drain the pool, remove or reconstruct the Roman pipes, and the building will stand."

"Is that all?" asked the duke, disappointment in his voice. "I thought that you might say the red was the Lady Renwein's soldiers, the white mine or some such."

"Dreams are never quite so obvious, my lord. They are devious messages to us, truth . . ." he paused for a moment and put his hands on Merlin's shoulders, "truth on the slant."

Lady Reinwein was nodding. "Yes, that would make sense. About the drains and the Roman pipes, I mean. Not the dream. You need not have used so much folderol in order to give us good advice."

Ambrosius smiled and stepped away from Merlin and made another deep bow. "But my lady, who would have listened to a traveling magician on matters of . . . shall we say . . . state?"

She smiled back.

"And besides," Ambrosius added, "I had not heard this dream until this very moment. I had given no thought before it to your palace or anything else of Carmarthen excepting the fair. It is the boy's dream that tells us what to do. And, unlike his mother of blessed memory, I could never guess a baby's sex before it was born lest she dreamed it. And she, the minx, never mentioned that she was carrying a boy to me, nor did she dream of him till after he was born when she, dying, spoke of him once. 'He will be a hawk among princes,' she said. So I named him Merlin."

It was two days later when a special messenger came to the green wagon with a small casket filled with coins and a small gold dragon with a faceted red jewel for an eye.

"Her ladyship sends these with her compliments," said the soldier who brought the casket. "There was indeed a hidden pool beneath the foundation. And the pipes, which were as gray and speckled and grained as eggs, were rotted through. In some places they were gnawed on, too, by some small underground beasts. Her lady begs you to stay or at least send the boy back to her for yet another dream."

Ambrosius accepted the casket solemnly, but shook his head. "Tell her ladyship that—alas—there is but one dream per prince. And we must away. The fair here is done and there is another holy day fair in Londinium, many days journey from here. Even with such a prize as her lady has gifted us, Ambrosius the Wandering Mage and his company can never be still long." He bowed.

But Ambrosius did not proffer the real reason they were away: that a kind of restless fear drove him on, for after the performance when they were back in the wagon, Merlin had cried out against him. "But that was not the true meaning of the dream. There *will* be fighting here—the red dragon of the Britons and the Saxon white will fight again. The tower is only a small part—of the dream, of the whole."

And Ambrosius had sighed loudly then, partly for effect, and said, "My dear son, for as I claimed you, now you are mine forever, magecraft is a thing of the eye and ear. You tell me that what you dream comes true—but on the slant. And I say that to tell a prince to his face that you have dreamed of his doom invites the dreamer's doom as well. And, as you yourself reminded me, it may not be *all* the truth. The greatest wisdom of any dreamer is to survive in order to dream again. Besides, how do you really know if what you dream is true or if, in the telling of it, you make it come true? We are men, not beasts, because we can dream and because we can make those dreams come true."

Merlin had closed his eyes then, and when he opened them again, they were the clear vacant blue of a newborn babe. "Father," he had said, and it was a child's voice speaking.

Ambrosius had shivered with the sound of it, for he knew that sons in the natural order of things o'erthrew their fathers when they came of age. And Merlin, it was clear, was very quick to learn and quicker to grow.

"Sir," said Merlin, "this is my desire: the first night that ye shall lie by Igraine ye shall get a child on her, and when that is born, that it shall be delivered to me for to nourish there as I will have it; for it shall be your worship, and the child's avail as mickle as the child is worth."

"I will well," said the king, "as thou wilt have it."

"Now make you ready," said Merlin, "this night ye shall lie with Igraine in the castle of Tintagil; and ye shall be like the duke her husband. . . ."

—Le Morte D'Arthur
by Sir Thomas Malory

The Annunciation

Do not hate me,
sweet Igraine,
for the likeness
who has lain
this cloudy night
belly to back,
for he has what
dead men all lack.
He has the passion
and the seed,

and shadows can
no longer breed.

Love goes in motley
and in mask
and, counterfeit,
completes the task
that I have set him
for this night.
So love plays love
without the light.

Do you think I am
passion's Fool
to simulate
the lover's tool?
I am the man
masked by your side,
you are *my* all
unwitting bride.

Touch him sweetly,
sweet Igraine,
that this knight
might prove again
that love lasts longest
where love longs most.
Your womb will house
a mighty host.

I swear—and do not
take it light—
to bear the burden
of this night,
and in my arms
the child shall live

that has the greatest
gift to give:
this god's son will
redeem the land.
All this, this night,
I have long planned.

So sleep and sweetly,
sweet Igraine,
such loving will not
come again
when man and mage
are so entwined
in hand and heart
and loin and mind.

"It is well done," said Merlin, "that ye take a wife, for a man of your bounty and noblesse should not be without a wife. Now is there any that ye love more than another?"

"Yea," said King Arthur, "I love Guenever the king's daughter, Leodegrance of the land of Cameliard, the which holdeth in his house the Table Round that ye told he had of my father Uther. And this damosel is the most valiant and fairest lady that I know living, or yet that ever I could find."

—Le Morte D'Arthur
by Sir Thomas Malory

The Gwynhfar

The *gwynhfar*—the white one, the pure one, the anointed one—waited. She had waited every day since her birth, it seemed, for this appointed time. Attended by her voiceless women in her underground rooms, the *gwynhfar's* limbs had been kept oiled, her bone-white hair had been cleaned and combed. No color was allowed to stain her dead-white cheeks, no *maurish* black to line her eyes. White as the day she had been born, white as the foam on a troubled sea, white as the lilybell grown in the wood, she waited.

Most of her life had been spent on her straw bed in that half-sleep nature spent on her. She moved from small dream to small dream, moment to moment, hour to hour, day to

day, without any real knowledge of what awaited her. Nor
did she care. The *gwynhfar* did not have even creature sense,
nor had she been taught to think. All she had been taught
was waiting. It was her duty, it was her life.

She had been the firstborn of a dour landholder and his
wife. Pulled silently from between her mother's thighs,
bleached as bone, her tiny eyes closed tight against the
agonizing light, the *gwynhfar* cried only in the day—a high,
thin, mewling call. At night, without the sun to torment
her, she seemed content; she waited.

They say now that the old mage attended her birth, but
that is not true. He did not come for weeks, even months,
till word of the white one's birth had traveled mouth to ear,
mouth to ear, over and over the intervening miles. He did
not come at first, but his messengers came, as they did to
every report of a marvel. They had visited two-headed calves,
fish-scaled infants, and twins joined at the hip and heart.
When they heard of the white one, they came to her, too.

She waited for them as she waited for everything else.

And when the messengers saw that the stories were true
enough, they reported back to the stone hall. So the Old
One himself came, wrapped in his dignity and the sour
trappings of state.

He had to bend down to enter the cottage, for age had
not robbed him of the marvelous height that had first brought
him to the attention of the Oldest Ones, those who dwell
in the shadows of the Circle of Stones. He bent and bent
till it seemed he would bend quite in two, and still he broke
his head on the lintel.

"A marvel," it was said. "The blood anointed the door."
That was no marvel, but a failing of judgment and the blood
a mere trickle where the skin broke apart. But that is what
was said. What the Old One himself said was in a language
far older than he and twice as filled with power. But no one
reported *it*, for who but the followers of the oldest way even
know that tongue?

As the Old One stood there, gazing at the mewling white
babe in her half sleep before the flickering fire, he nodded
and stroked his thin beard. This, too, they say, and I have
seen him often enough musing in just that way, so it could
have been so.

Then he stretched forth his hand, that parchment-colored, five-fingered magician's wand that could make balls and cards and silken banners disappear. He stretched forth his hand and touched the child. She shivered and woke fully for the first time, gazing at a point somewhere beyond his hand but not as far as his face with her watery pink eyes.

"So," he said in that nasal excuse for a voice. "So." He was never profligate with words. But it was enough.

The landholder gladly gave up the child, grateful to have the monster from his hearth. Sons could help till the lands. Only the royals crave girls. They make good counters in the bargaining games played across the castle boundary lines. But this girl was not even human enough to cook and clean and wipe the bottoms of her sisters and brothers to come. The landholder would have killed the moon-misbegotten thing on its emergence from his child-bride's womb had not the midwife stayed him. He sold the child for a single gold piece and thought himself clever in the bargain.

And did the Old One clear his throat then and consecrate their trade with words? Did he speak of prophesy or pronounce upon omens? If the landholder's wife had hoped for such to ease her guilt, she got short shrift of him. He had paid with a coin and a single syllable.

"So," he had said. And so it was.

The Old One carried the *gwynhfar* back over the miles with his own hands. *"With his own hands,"* run the wonder tales, as if this were an awesome thing, carrying a tiny, witless babe. But think on it. Would he have trusted her to another, having come so far, across the years and miles, to find her? Would he have given her into clumsier hands when his own could still pull uncooked eggs from his sleeves without a crack or a drop?

Behind him, they say, came his people: the priests and the seers, a grand processional. But I guess rather he came by himself and at night. She would have been a noisy burden to carry through the bright, scalding light; squalling and squealing at the sun. The moon always quieted her. Besides, he wanted to surprise them with her, to keep her to himself till the end. For was it not written that the *gwynhfar* would arise and bind the kingdom:

> *Gwynhfar,* white as bone,
> Shall make the kingdom one.

Just as it had been written in the entrails of deer and the
bloody leavings of carrion crow that the Tall One, blessed
be, would travel the length of the kingdom to find her.
Miracles are made by hands such as his, and prophesies can
be invented.

And then, too, he would want to be sure. He would want
time to think about what he carried, that small, white-haired
marvel, that unnature. For if the Old One was anything, he
was a planner. If he had been born better, he would have
been a mighty king. So, wrapped in the cloak of night,
keeping the babe from her enemy light, which drained even
the small strength she had, and scheming—always scheming—the Old One moved through the land.

By day, of course, there would have been no mistaking
him. His height ever proclaimed him. Clothes were no dis-
guise. A mask but pointed the finger. At night, though, he
was only a long shadow in a world of long shadows.

I never saw him then, but I know it all. I can sort through
stories as a crow pecks through grain. And though it is said
he rode a whirlwind home, it was a time of year for storms.
They were no worse than other years. It is just that legend
has a poor memory, and hope an even worse.

The Old One returned with a cough that wracked his
long, thin body and an eye scratched out by a tree limb.
The black patch he wore thereafter gave rise to new tales.
They say he had been blinded in one eye at his first sight
of her, the *gwynhfar*. But I have it from the physician who
attended him that there was a great scar on his cheek and
splinters still in the flesh around the eye.

And what did the Old One say of the wound?

"Clean it," he said. And then, "So!" There is no story
there. That is why words of power have been invented for
him.

The Old One had a great warren built for the child under
the ground so the light would not disturb her rest. Room
upon room was filled with things for a growing princess,
but nothing there to speak to a child. How could he know
what would interest a young one? It was said he had never

been a babe. This was only partly a lie. He had been raised
by the Oldest Ones himself. He had been young but he had
never had a youth. So he waited impatiently for her to grow.
He wanted to watch the unfolding of this white, alien flower,
his only child.

But the *gwynhfar* was slow. Slow to sit, slow to crawl,
slow to eat. Like a great white slug, she never did learn
speech or to hold her bowels. She had to be kept wrapped
in swaddling under her dresses to keep her clean, but who
could see through the silk to know? She grew bigger but
not much older, both a natural and unnatural thing. So she
was never left alone.

It meant that the Old One had to change his plan. And
so his plan became this. He had her beaten every day, but
never badly. And on a signal, he would enter her underground chambers and put an end to her punishment. Again
and again he arrived just as blood was about to be drawn.
Then he would send away her tormentors, calling down
horrid punishments upon them. It was not long before the
gwynhfar looked only to him. She would turn that birch-
white face toward the door waiting for him to enter, her
watery eyes glistening. The over-big head on the weak neck
seemed to strain for his words, though it was clear soon
enough that she was deaf as well.

If he could have found another as white as she, he would
likely have gotten rid of her. Perhaps. But there have been
stranger loves. And only he could speak to her, a language
of simple hand signs and finger plays. As she grew into
womanhood, the two would converse in a limited fashion.
It was some relief from statecraft and magecraft and the
tortuous imaginings of history.

On those days and weeks when he did not come to see
her, the *gwynhfar* often fell into a half sleep. She ate when
fed, roused to go out into the night only when pulled from
her couch. The women around her kept her exercised as if
she were some exotic, half-wild beast, but they did take
good care of her. They guessed what would happen if they
did not.

What they did not guess was that they were doomed
anyway. Her raising was to be the Old One's secret. Only
one woman, who escaped with a lover, told what really

happened. No one ever believed her, not even her lover,
and he was soon dead in a brawl and she with him.

But I believed. I am bound to believe what cannot be
true, to take fact from fancy, fashion fancy from fact.

The plan was changed, but not the promise.

> *Gwynhfar,* white as bone,
> Shall make the kingdom one.

The rhyme was known, sung through the halls of power
and along the muddy country lanes. Not a man or woman
or child but wished it to be so: for the kingdom to be bound
up, its wounds cleansed. Justice is like a round banquet
table—it comes full circle, and none should be higher or
lower than the next. So the mage waited, for the *gwynhfar's*
first signs of womanhood. And the white one waited for the
dark prince she had been promised, light and dark, two
sides of the same coin. She of the old tribes, he of the new.
She of the old faith and he of the new. He listened to new
advisers, men of action, new gods. She had but one adviser,
knew no action, had one god. That was the promise: old
and new wedded together. How else can a kingdom be made
one?

How did the mage tell her this, finger upon finger? Did
she understand? I only know she waited for the day with
the patience of the dreamer, with the solidity of a stone.
For that was what she was, a white pebble in a rushing
stream, which does not move but changes the direction of
the water that passes over it.

I know the beginning of the tale, but not yet the end.
Perhaps this time the wisdom of the Oldest Ones will mis-
carry. Naught may come of naught. Such miracles are often
barren. There have been rumors of white ones before. Beasts
sometimes bear them. But they are weak, they die young,
they cannot conceive. A queen without issue is a dreadful
thing. Unnatural.

And the mage has planned it all except for the dark
prince. He is a young bear of a king and I think will not
be bought so easily with handwrought miracles. His hunger
for land and for women, his need for heirs, will not be

checked by the mage's blanched and barren offering. He is, I fear, of a lustier mind.

And I? I am no one, a singer of songs, a teller of tales. But I am the one to be wary of, for I remake the past and call it truth. I leave others to the rote of history, which is dry, dull, and unbelievable. Who is to say which mouth's outpourings will lift the soul higher—that which *is* or that which *could be?* Did it really flood, or did Noah have a fine storymaker living in his house? I care not either way. It is enough for me to sing.

But stay. It is my turn on the boards. Watch. I stride to the room's center, where the song's echo will linger longest. I lift my hands toward the young king, toward the old mage, toward the *gwynhfar* swaddled in silk who waits, as she waits for everything else. I bow my head and raise my voice.

"Listen," I say, my voice low and cozening. "Listen, lords and ladies, as I sing of the coming days. I sing of the time when the kingdom will be one. And I call my song, the lay of the dark King Artos and of Guinevere the Fair."

"Well," said Merlin, "I know a lord of yours in this
land, that is a passing true man and a faithful, and
he shall have the nourishing of your child; and his
name is Sir Ector, and he is a lord of fair livelihood
in many parts in England and Wales; and this lord,
Sir Ector, let him be sent for, for to come and speak
with you, and desire him yourself, as he loveth you,
that he will put his own child to nourishing to another
woman, and that his wife nourish yours. . . ."

—Le Morte D'Arthur
by Sir Thomas Malory

The
Dragon's Boy

It was on a day in early spring with the clouds scudding across a gray sky, that the boy found the cave. He had been chasing after Lord Ector's brachet hound, the one who always slipped her chain to go after hare. She had slipped him as well, leaving him lost in the boggy wasteland north of the castle walls. He had crossed and recrossed a small, meandering stream following her, wading thigh-deep in water that—he was painfully aware of it—would only come up to the other boys' knees. The reminder of his height only made him crankier.

The sun was high, his stomach empty, and the brachet had quit baying an hour earlier. She was no doubt back at the kennel yard, slopping up her food. But she was his responsibility, and he had to stay out until he was sure. Besides, he was lost. Well, not exactly lost but *bothered* a bit, which was a phrase he had picked up from the master of hounds, a whey-colored man for all that he was out of doors most of the day.

The boy looked around for a place to get out of the noon sun, for the low, hummocky swamp with its brown pools and quaking mosses offered little shelter. And then he saw a small tor mounding up over the bog. He decided to climb it a bit to see if he could find a place where he might shelter, maybe even survey the land. He'd never been quite this far from the castle on his own before and certainly had never come out into the northern fens where the peat-hags reigned, and he needed time to think about the way home. And the brachet. If the mound had been higher, he wouldn't have attempted it. The High Tor, the really large mount northwest of the manor, had somewhat of an evil reputation. But this hillock was hardly that. He needed to get his bearings and sight the castle walls or at least a tower.

He was halfway up the tor when he saw the cave.

It was only an unprepossessing black hole in the rock, as round as if it had been carved and then smoothed by a master hand. He stepped in, being careful of the long, spear-like, hanging rocks, and let his eyes get used to the dark. Only then did he hear the breathing. It was not very loud, but it was steady and rumbling, with an occasional *pop!* that served as punctuation.

He held his breath and began to back out of the cave, hit his head on something that rang in twenty different tones, and said a minor curse under his breath.

"Staaaaaaaaaaay," came a low command.

He stopped. And so, for a stuttering moment, did his heart.

"Whoooooooooooo are you?" It was less an echo bouncing off cave walls than an elongated sigh.

The boy bit his lip and answered in a voice that broke several times in odd places. "I am nobody. Just Artos. A fosterling from the castle." Then he added hastily, "Sir."

A low rumbling sound, more like a snore than a sentence,

was all that was returned to him. It was that homey sound which freed him of his terror long enough to ask, "And who are you?" He hesitated. "Sir."

Something creaked. There was a strange clanking. Then the voice, augmented almost tenfold, boomed at him, "I am the Great Riddler. I am the Master of Wisdoms. I am the Word and I am the Light. I Was and Am and Will Be."

Artos nearly fainted from the noise. He put his right hand before him as if to hold back the sound. When the echoes had ended, he said in a quiet little voice, "Are you a hermit, sir? An anchorite? Are you a Druid? A penitent knight?"

The great whisper that answered him came in a rush of wind. "I am the Dragon."

"Oh," said Artos.

"Is that all you can say?" asked the dragon. "I tell you I am the Dragon and all you can answer is *oh?*"

The boy was silent.

The great breathy voice sighed. "Sit down, boy. It has been a long time since I have had company in my cave. A long time and a lonely time."

"But . . . but . . . but." It was not a good beginning.

"No *buts,*" said the dragon.

"But . . ." Artos began again, needing greatly to uphold his end of the conversation.

"Shush, boy, and listen. I will pay for your visit."

The boy sat. It was not greed that stayed him. Rather, he was comforted by the thought that he was not to be eaten.

"So, Artos, how would you like your payment? In gold, in jewels, or in wisdom?"

A sudden flame from the center of the cave lit up the interior and, for the first time, Artos could see that there were jewels scattered about the floor as thick as pebbles. But dragons were known to be great games players. Cunning, like an old habit, claimed the boy. Like most small people, he had a genius for escape. "Wisdom, sir," he said.

Another bright flame spouted from the cave center. "An excellent choice," said the dragon. "I've been needing a boy just your age to pass my wisdom on to. So listen well."

Artos did not move and hoped that the dragon would see by his attitude that he was listening.

"My word of wisdom for the day is this: Old dragons, like old thorns, can still prick. And I am a very old dragon. Take care."

"Yes, sir," said Artos, thinking but not saying that that was a bit of wit often spoken on the streets of the village nestled inside the castle walls. But the warning by the villagers was of priests and thorns, not dragons. Aloud he said, "I will remember. Sir."

"Go now," said the dragon. "And as a reward for being such a good listener, you may take that small jewel. There." The strange clanking that Artos had heard before accompanied the extension of a gigantic foot with four enormous toes, three in the front and one in the back. It scrabbled along the cave floor, then stopped not far from Artos. Then the nail from the center toe extended peculiarly and tapped on a red jewel the size of a leek bulb.

Artos moved cautiously toward the jewel and the claw. Hesitating a moment, he suddenly leaned over and grabbed up the jewel. Then he scuttered back to the cave entrance.

"I will expect you tomorrow," said the dragon. "You will come during your time off."

"How did you know I had time off?" asked Artos.

"When you have become as wise as a dragon, you will know these things."

Artos sighed.

"There is a quick path from the back bridge. Discover it. And you will bring me stew. With *meat!*" The nail was suddenly sheathed and, quite rapidly, the foot was withdrawn into the dark center of the cave.

"To—tomorrow," promised the boy, not meaning a word of it.

The next morning at the smithy, caught in the middle of a quarrel between Old Linn the apothecary and Magnus Pieter the swordmaker, Artos was reminded of his promise. He had not forgotten the dragon—indeed the memory of the great clanking scales, the giant claw, the shaft of searing breath, the horrendous whisper had haunted his dreams. But he had quite conveniently forgotten his promise, or shunted it aside, or buried it behind layers of caution, until the argument had broken out.

"But there is never any *meat* in my gravy," whined Old Linn.

"Nor any meat in your manner," replied the brawny smith. "Nor were you mete for battle." The smith rather fancied himself a wordsman as well as a swordsman. And until Old Linn had had a fit, falling face first into his soup in the middle of entertaining the visiting High King, the smith had been spitted regularly by Old Linn's quick tongue. Now Linn was too slow for such ragging and he never told tales after meals anymore. It was said he had lost the heart for it after his teeth had left prints on the table. But he was kept on at the castle because Lord Ector had a soft heart and a long memory. And because—so backstair gossip had it—Linn had a cupboard full of strange herbs locked up behind doors covered with deep carved runes.

Artos, who had been at the smithy to try and purchase a sword with his red jewel, was caught with his bargaining only just begun. He had not even had time to show the gem to Magnus Pieter when Old Linn had shambled in and, without any prelude, started his whining litany. His complaints were always laid at the smith's door. No one else in the castle was as old as the pair of them. They were best of friends by their long and rancorous association.

"My straw is ne'er changed but once a se'nnight," Linn complained. "My slops are ne'er emptied. I am given the dregs of the wine to drink. And now I must sit, if I am to be welcomed at all, well below the salt."

The smith smiled and returned to tapping on his piece of steel. He had stopped when Artos had begun his inquiries. In time to the beat of the hammer, he said, "But you have straw, though you no longer earn it. And a pot for your slops, which you can empty yourself. You have wine, even though you ne'er pay for it. And even below the salt, there is gravy in your bowl."

That was when Old Linn had whined piteously, "But there is never any *meat* in my gravy."

It was the word *meat* and Magnus Pieter's seven or eight variations on it, that rung like a knell in Artos' head. For *meat* had been the dragon's final word.

He slunk off without even the promise of a sword, that shining piece of steel that might make him an equal in the

eyes of the other boys, the gem still burning brightly in his
tightly clenched hand.

He brought a small pot of gravy with three pieces of
meat with him. Strolling casually out the back gate as if he
had all the time in the world, nodding slightly at the guards
over the portcullis, Artos could feel his heartbeat quicken.
He had walked rather more quickly over the moat bridge,
glancing at the gray-green water where the old moat tortoise
lazed atop the rusted crown of a battle helm. Once he was
across, he began to run.

It was difficult not to spill the stew, but he managed.
The path was a worn thread through a wilderness of peat-
mosses and tangled brush. He even clambered over two
rock outcroppings in the path that were studded with stones
that looked rather like lumps of meat themselves. And actually climbing over the rocks was easier than wheedling
the pot of stew had been. He only had it because Mag the
scullery was sweet on him and he had allowed her to kiss
him full on the lips. She hadn't noticed how he had held
his breath, hoping to avoid the stink of her garlic, and closed
his eyes not to see her bristly mustache. And she sighed so
much after the kiss she hadn't had time to ask what he
needed the stew for. But what if the dragon wanted gravy
every day and he had to give Mag more kisses. It didn't
bear thinking about, so Artos thought instead about the path.
The dragon had been right. There was a quicker route back
to the mount. Its only disadvantages were the two large
rocks and the old thorny briar bushes. But they, at least,
were safer than the peat pools which held bones enough
way far down.

He got to the cave rather quicker than he had bargained.
Breathless, he squinted into the dark hole. This time he
heard no heavy dragon breathing.

"Maybe," he said aloud to himself, his own voice lending
him badly needed courage, "there's no one home. So I can
just leave the gravy—and go."

"Staaaaaaaaay," came the sudden rumbling.

Artos almost dropped the pot.

"I have the gravy," he shouted quickly. He hadn't meant
to be so loud, but fear always made him either too quiet or

too loud. He was never sure which it was to be.

"Then give it meeeeeeeee," said the voice, followed by the clanking as the great claw extended halfway into the cave.

Artos could tell it was the foot by its long shadow. This time there was no stream of fire, only a hazy smoldering light from the back of the cave. Feeling a little braver then, he said, "I shall need to take the pot back with me. Sir."

"You shall take a bit of wisdom instead," came the voice.

Artos wondered if it would make him wise enough to avoid Mag's sweaty embrace. Somehow he doubted it.

"Tomorrow you shall have the pot. When you bring me more."

"More?" This time Artos' voice squeaked.

"Mooooooooore," said the dragon. "With meat!" The nail extended, just as it had the day before, and caught under the pot handle. There was a horrible screeching as the pot was lifted several inches into the air, then slowly withdrawn into the recesses of the cave. There were strange scrabbling noises as if the dragon were sorting through its possessions, and then the clanking resumed. The claw returned and dropped something at Artos' feet.

He looked down. It was a book, rather tatty around the edges, he thought, though in the cave light it was hard to be sure.

"Wissssssssdom," said the dragon.

Artos shrugged. "It's just a book. I know my letters. Father Bertram taught me."

"Letterssssssss turn matter into ssssssspirit," hissed the dragon.

"You mean it's a book of magic?"

"All booksssssss are magic, boy." The dragon sounded just a bit cranky.

"Well, I can read," said Artos, stooping to pick up the book. He added a quick, "Thank you," thinking he should seem grateful. *Old thorns and old dragons* . . . he reminded himself.

"You can read *letters,* my boy, which is more than I can say for your castle contemporaries. And you can read *words.* But you must learn to read *inter linea,* between the lines."

Edging backward to the cave's mouth, Artos opened the

book and scanned the first page. His fingers underlined each word, his mouth formed them. He turned the page. Then he looked up puzzled. "There is nothing written between the lines. Sir."

Something rather like a chuckle crossed with a cough echoed from the cave. "There is always something written between the lines. But it takes great wisdom to read it."

"Then why me, sir? I have little wisdom."

"Because . . . because you are here."

"Here?"

"Today. And not back at Ector's feeding his brachet or cleaning out the mews or sweating in the smithy or fighting with that pack of unruly boys. Here. For the getting of wisdom." The dragon made stretching noises.

"Oh."

There was a sudden tremendous wheezing and clanking and a strange, "Oh-oh," from the dragon.

Artos peered into the back of the cave nervously. It was all darkness and shadow and an occasional finger of firelight. "Are you all right? Sir?"

A long silence followed during which Artos wondered whether he should go to the dragon. He wondered if he had even the smallest amount of wisdom needed to help out. Then, just as he was about to make the plunge, the dragon's voice came hissing back. "Yessssss, boy."

"Yes what, sir?"

"Yesssssss I am all right."

"Well, then," said Artos, putting one foot quietly behind the other, "thank you for my wisdom."

A furious flame spat across the cave, leaping through the darkness to lick Artos' feet. He jumped back, startled at the dragon's accuracy and suddenly hideously afraid. Had it just been preparation for the dragon's dinner after all? He suddenly wished for the sword he had not yet purchased, turned, and ran out of the cave.

The dragon's voice followed him. "Sssssssssilly child. That was not the wisdom."

From a safe place alongside the outside wall of the cave, Artos peeked in. "There's more?" he asked.

"By the time I am through with you, Artos Pendragon, Arthur son of the dragon, you will read *inter linea* in people as well." There was a loud moan and another round of furious clanking, and then total silence.

Taking it as a dismissal and holding the book hard against his chest, Artos ran down the hill. Whatever else he thought about as he neared the castle walls, topmost in his mind was what he would tell Mag about the loss of the gravy pot. It might mean another kiss. That was the fell thought that occupied him all the way home.

Artos could not read the book without help, he knew it at once. The sentences were much too long and interspersed with Latin and other languages. Perhaps that was the between lines the dragon had meant. The only help available was Old Linn, and he did not appear until well after dinner. Unfortunately, that was the time that Artos was the busiest, feeding the dogs, checking the jesses on the hawks, cleaning the smithy. Father Bertram might have helped had he still been alive, though somehow Artos doubted it. The dragon's book was neither Testament nor Commentary, that much he *could* read, and the good father had been fierce about what he had considered proper fare. The castle bonfires had often burned texts of which he disapproved. Even Lady Marion's *Book of Hours,* which had taken four scribes the full part of a year to set down, had gone up in Father Bertram's righteous flames because Adam and Eve had no fig leaves. This Artos had on good authority, though he had never seen it himself, for Lady Marion had complained to Lady Sylvia who had tittered about it to her serving girls who had passed the news along with the gravy to young Cai who had mentioned it as a joke to his friends in the cow shed when Artos, who had been napping in the haymow, overheard them.

No, the good Father Bertram would never have helped. Old Linn, though, was different. He could read four tongues well: English, Latin, Greek, and bardic runes. It was said his room was full of books. He could recite the "Conception of Pyrderi," a tale Artos loved for the sheer sound of it, and the stories about the children of Llyr and the Cauldron and the Iron House and the horse made for Bran. Or at least Linn used to be able to tell them all. Before he had been taken ill so suddenly and dramatically, his best piece had always been the "Battle of the Trees." Artos could not remember a time when dinners of great importance at the castle had not ended with Linn's declaiming of it. In fact, Lord Ector's Irish retainers called Linn *shanachie* which, as far as Artos could tell from their garbled and endless explanations, simply meant "storyteller." But they said the word with awe when coupling it to Old Linn's name.

The problem, Artos thought, was that the old man hated him. Well, perhaps *hate* was too strong a word, but he seemed to prefer the young gentlemen of the house, not the impoverished fosterling. Linn especially lavished attention on Sir Cai who, as far as Artos was concerned, long ago let his muscles o'ertake his head. And Sir Bedvere, slack jawed and hardhanded. And Sir Lancot, the pretty boy. Once Artos, too, had tried to curry favor with the trio of lordlings, fetching and carrying and helping them with their schoolwork. But then they all grew up, and the three grew up faster and taller and louder. And once Sir Lancot as a joke had pulled Artos' pants down around his ankles in the courtyard and the other two called out the serving maids to gawk. And that led to Mag's getting sweet on him, which was why he had grown to despise Mag and pity the boys, even though they were older and bigger and better placed than he.

Still, there was a time for putting aside such feelings, thought Artos. The getting of wisdom was surely such a time. He would need help in reading the dragon's book. None of the others, Cai or Bedvere or Lancot, could read half as well as he. They could only just make out the prayers in their psalters. Sir Ector could not read at all. So it would have to be Old Linn.

But to his despair, the apothecary could not be found after dinner. In desperation, he went to talk to the old man's best friend, the smith.

"Come now, young Art," called out Magnus Pieter as Artos approached the smithy. "Did we not have words just yesterday? Something about a sword and a stone?"

Artos tried to think of a way to get the conversation around to Linn's whereabouts, but the conversation would not move at his direction. The smith willed it where he would. At last there was nothing left to do but remove the leathern bag from around his neck and take out the jewel.

He dropped it onto the anvil. It made a funny little pinging sound.

Magnus sucked on his lower lip and snorted through his nose. "By God, boy, and where'd you get that stone?"

To tell the truth meant getting swat for a liar. He suddenly realized it would be the same if he showed the book to Linn. So he lied. "I was left it by . . . Father Bertram," he said. "And I've. . . ." the lies came slowly. He was, by inclination, an honest boy. He preferred silence to an untruth.

"Kept it till now, have you?" asked the smith. "Well, well, and of course you have. After all, there's not much in that village of ours to spend such a jewel on."

Artos nodded silently, thankful to have Magnus Pieter do the lying for him.

"And what would you be wanting for such a jewel?" asked the smith with the heavy-handed jocularity he always confused with cunning.

Knowing that he must play the innocent in order to get the better bargain, Artos said simply, "Why, a sword, of course."

"Of course!" Magnus Pieter laughed, hands on hips, throwing his head way back.

Since the other smiths he had known laughed in just that way, Artos assumed it was something taught.

The smith stopped laughing and cocked his head to one side. "Well?"

"I am old enough to have a sword of my own," said Artos. "And now I can pay for a good one."

"How good?" asked the smith in his heavy manner.

Artos knelt before the anvil and the red jewel was at the level of his eyes. As if he were addressing the stone and not the smith, he chanted a bit from a song Old Linn used to sing:

> *"And aye their swordes soe sore can byte,*
> *Throughe help of gramarye . . ."*

From behind him the smith sighed. "Aye," the old man said, "and a good sword it shall be. A fine blade, a steel of power. And while I make it for you, young poet, you must think of a good name for your sword from this stone."

He reached across Artos' shoulder and plucked up the jewel, holding it high over both their heads.

Artos stood slowly, never once taking his eyes from the jewel. For a moment he thought he saw dragon fire leaping and crackling there. Then he remembered the glowing coals of the forge. The stone reflected that, nothing more.

"Perhaps," he said, thinking out loud, "perhaps I shall call it Inter Linea."

The smith smiled. "Fine name, that. Makes me think of foreign climes." He pocketed the stone and began to work. Artos turned and left, for he had chores to do in the mews.

Each day that followed meant another slobbery kiss from Mag and another pot of stew. It seemed to Artos a rather messy prelude to wisdom. But after a week of it, he found the conversations with the dragon worth the mess.

The dragon spoke knowingly of other lands where men walked on their heads instead of feet. Of lands down beneath the sea where the bells rang in underwater churches with each passing wave. It taught Artos riddles and their answers, like

> As round as an apple, as deep as a cup,
> And all the king's horses can't pull it up,

which was "a well," of course.

And it sang him ballads from the prickly, gorse-covered land of the Scots who ran naked and screaming into battle. And songs from the cold, icy Norsemen who prowled in their dragon ships. And love songs from the silk-and-honey lands of Araby.

And once the dragon taught him a trick with pots and jewels, clanking and creaking noisily all the while, its huge foot mixing up the pots till Artos' head fair ached to know under which one lay the emerald as big as an egg. And that game he had used later with Lancot and Bedvere and Cai and won from them a number of gold coins till they threatened him. With his promised new sword he might have beaten them, but not with his bare hands. So he used a small man's wiles to trick them once again, picked up the winnings, and left them grumbling over the cups and peas he had used for the game.

And so day by day, week by week, month by month, Artos gained wisdom.

It took three tries and seven months before Artos had his sword. Each new steel had something unacceptable about it. The first had a hilt that did not sit comfortably in his hand. Bedvere claimed it instead, and Magnus Pieter was so pleased with the coins Sir Bedvere paid it was weeks before he was ready to work on another. Instead he shoed horses, made latches and a gigantic candelabrum for the dining room to Lady Marion's specifications.

The second sword had a strange crossbar that the smith swore would help protect the hand. Artos thought the sword unbalanced but Cai, who prized newness over all things, insisted that he wanted that blade. Again Magnus Pieter was pleased enough to spend the weeks following making farm implements like plowshares and hoes.

The third sword was still bright with its tempering when Lancot claimed it.

"Cai and Bedvere have new swords," Lancot said, his handsome face drawn down with longing. He reached his hand out.

Artos, who had been standing in the shadows of the smithy, was about to say something when Old Linn hobbled in. His mouth and hair spoke of a lingering illness, both being yellowed and lifeless. But his voice was strong.

"You were always a man true to his word," he reminded the smith.

"And true to my swords," said Magnus Pieter, pleased with the play.

Artos stepped from the shadows then and held out his hand. The smith put the sword in it and Artos turned it this way and that to catch the light. The watering on the blade made a strange pattern that looked like the flame from a dragon's mouth. It sat well and balanced in his hand.

"He likes the blade," said Old Linn.

Magnus Pieter shrugged, smiling.

Artos turned to thank the apothecary but he was gone and so was Lancot. When he peered out the smithy door, there were the two of them walking arm and arm up the winding path toward the castle.

"So you've got your Inter Linea now," said the smith. "And about time you took one. Nothing wrong with the other two."

"And you got a fine price for them," Artos said.

The smith returned to his anvil and the clang of hammer on new steel ended their conversation.

Artos ran out of the castle grounds, hallooing so loudly even the tortoise dozing on the rusted helm lifted its sleepy head. He fairly leapt over the two rocks in the path. They seemed to have gotten smaller with each trip to the dragon's lair. He was calling still when he approached the entrance to the cave.

"Ho, old flame-tongue," he cried out, the sword allowing him his first attempt at familiarity. "Furnace-lung, look what I have. My sword. From the stone you gave me. It is a rare beauty."

There was no answer.

Suddenly afraid that he had overstepped the bounds and that the dragon lay sulking within, Artos peered inside.

The cave was dark, cold, silent.

Slowly Artos walked in and stopped about halfway. He felt surrounded by the icy silence. But that was all. There was no sense of dragon there. No presence.

"Sir? Father dragon? Are you home?" He put a hand up to one of the hanging stones to steady himself. In the complete dark he had little sense of what was up and what was down.

Then he laughed. "Oh, I know, you have gone out on a flight." It was the only answer that came to him, though the dragon had never once mentioned flying. But everyone knows dragons have wings. And wings mean flight. Artos laughed again, a hollow little chuckle. Then he turned toward the small light of the cave entrance. "I'll come back tomorrow. At my regular time," he called over his shoulder. He said it out loud just in case the dragon's magic extended to retrieving words left in the still cave air. "Tomorrow," Artos promised.

* * *

But the pattern had been altered subtly and, like a weaving gone awry, could not be changed back to the way it had been without a weakness in the cloth.

The next day Artos did not go to the cave. Instead he practiced swordplay with willow wands in the main courtyard, beating Cai soundly and being beaten in turn by both Bedvere and Lancot.

The following morn, he and the three older boys were sent by Lady Marion on a fortnight's journey to gather gifts of jewels and silks from the market towns for the coming holy days. Some at Ector's castle celebrated the solstice with the Druids, some kept the holy day for the Christ child's birth, and a few of the old soldiers still drank bull's blood and spoke of Mithras in secret meetings under the castle, for there was a vast warren of halls and rooms there. But they all gave gifts to one another at the year's turning, whichever gods they knelt to.

It was Artos' first such trip. The other boys had gone the year before under Linn's guidance. This year the four of them were given leave to go alone. Cai was so pleased he forgave Artos for the beating. Suddenly, they were the best of friends. And Bedvere and Lancot, who had beaten him, loved Artos now as well, for even when he had been on the ground with the wand at his throat and his face and arms red from the lashings, he had not cried "hold." There had been not even the hint of tears in his eyes. They admired him for that.

With his bright new sword belted at his side, brand-new leggings from the castle stores, and the new-sworn friends riding next to him, it was no wonder Artos forgot the dragon and the dark cave. Or, if he did not exactly forget, what he remembered was that the dragon hadn't been there when he wanted it the most. So, for a few days, for a fortnight, Artos felt he could, like Cai, glory in the new.

He did not glory in the dragon. It was old, old past counting the years, old past helping him, old and forgetful.

* * *

They came home with red rosy cheeks polished by the winter wind and bags packed with treasure. An extra two horses carried the overflow.

Cai, who had lain with his first girl, a serving wench of little beauty and great reputation, was full of new boasts. Bedvere and Lancot had won a junior tourney for boys under sixteen, Bedvere with his sword and Lancot the lance. And though Artos had been a favorite on the outbound trip, full of wonderful stories, riddles, and songs, as they turned toward home he had lapsed into long silences. By the time they were but a day's hard ride away, it was as if his mouth were bewitched.

The boys teased him, thinking it was Mag who worried him.

"Afraid of Old Garlic, then?" asked Cai. "At least Rosemary's breath was sweet." (Rosemary being the serving wench's name.)

"Or are you afraid of my sword?" said Bedvere.

"Or my lance?" Lancot added brightly.

When he kept silent, they tried to wheedle the cause of his set lips by reciting castle gossip. Every maiden, every alewife, every false nurse was named. Then they turned their attention to the men. They never mentioned dragons, though, for they did not know one lived by the castle walls. Artos had never told them of it.

But it was the dragon, of course, that concerned him. With each mile he remembered the darkness, the complete silence of the cave. At night he dreamed of it, the cave opening staring down from the hill like the empty eye socket of a long-dead beast.

They unpacked the presents carefully and carried them up to Lady Marion's quarters. She, in turn, fed them wine and cakes in her apartments, a rare treat. Her minstrel, a handsome boy except for his wandering left eye, sang a number of songs while they ate, even one in a Norman dialect. Artos drank only a single mouthful of the sweet wine. He ate nothing. He had heard all the songs before.

Thus it was well past sundown before Lady Marion let them go.

Artos would not join the others who were going to report

to Lord Ector. He pushed past Cai and ran down the stairs. The other boys called after him, but he ignored them. Only the startled ends of their voices followed him.

He hammered on the gate until the guards lifted the iron portcullis, then he ran across the moat bridge. Dark muddy lumps in the mushy ice were the only signs of life.

As he ran, he held his hand over his heart, cradling the two pieces of cake he had slipped into his tunic. Since he had had no time to beg stew from Mag, he hoped seed cakes would do instead. He did not, for a moment, believe the dragon had starved to death without his poor offering of stew. The dragon had existed many years before Artos had found the cave. It was not the *size* of the stew, but the *fact* of it.

He stubbed his toe on the second outcropping hard enough to force a small mewing sound from between his lips. The tor was icy and that made climbing it difficult. Foolishly he'd forgotten his gloves with his saddle gear. And he'd neglected to bring a light.

When he got to the mouth of the cave and stepped in, he was relieved to hear heavy breathing echoing off the cave wall, until he realized it was the sound of his own ragged breath.

"Dragon!" he cried out, his voice a misery.

Suddenly there was a small moan and an even smaller glow, like dying embers that have been breathed upon one last time.

"Is that you, my son?" The voice was scarcely a whisper, so quiet the walls could not find enough to echo.

"Yes, dragon," said Artos. "It is I."

"Did you bring me any stew?"

"Only two seed cakes."

"I like seed cakes."

"Then I'll bring them to you."

"Noooooooo." The sound held only the faintest memory of the powerful voice of before.

But Artos had already started toward the back of the cave, one hand in front to guide himself around the over-hanging rocks. He was halfway there when he stumbled against something and fell heavily to his knees. Feeling around, he touched a long, metallic curved blade.

"Has someone been here? Has someone tried to slay you?" he cried. Then, before the dragon could answer, Artos' hand traveled farther along the blade to its strange metallic base.

His hands told him what his eyes could not; his mouth spoke what his heart did not want to hear. "It is the dragon's foot."

He leaped over the metal construct and scrambled over a small rocky wall. Behind it, in the dying glow of a small fire, lay an old man on a straw bed. Near him were tables containing beakers full of colored liquids—amber, rose, green, and gold. On the wall were strange toothed wheels with handles.

The old man raised himself on one arm. "Pendragon," he said and tried to set his lips into a welcoming smile. "Son."

"Old Linn," replied Artos angrily, "I am no son of yours."

"There was once," the old man began quickly, settling into a story before Artos' anger had time to gel, "a man who would know Truth. And he traveled all over the land looking."

Without willing it, Artos was pulled into the tale.

"He looked along the seacoasts and in the quiet farm dales. He went into the country of lakes and across vast deserts seeking Truth. At last, one dark night in a small cave atop a hill, he found her. Truth was a wizened old woman with but a single tooth left in her head. Her eyes were rheumy. Her hair greasy strands. But when she called him into her cave, her voice was low and lyric and pure and that was how he knew he had found Truth."

Artos stirred uneasily.

The old man went on. "He stayed a year and a day by her side and learned all she had to teach. And when his time was done, he said, 'My Lady Truth, I must go back to my own home now. But I would do something for you in exchange.'" Linn stopped. The silence between them grew until it was almost a wall.

"Well, what did she say?" Artos asked at last.

"She told him, 'When you speak of me, tell your people that I am young and beautiful.'"

For a moment Artos said nothing. Then he barked out a

short, quick laugh. "So much for Truth."

Linn sat up and patted the mattress beside him, an invitation which Artos ignored. "Would you have listened these seven months to an old apothecary who had a tendency to fits?"

"You did not tell me the truth."

"I did not lie. You *are* the dragon's son."

Artos set his mouth and turned his back on the old man. His voice came out low and strained. *"I . . . am . . . not . . . your . . . son."*

"It is true that you did not spring from my loins," said the old man. "But I carried you here to Ector's castle and waited and hoped you would seek out my wisdom. But you longed for the truth of lance and sword. I did not have that to give." His voice was weak and seemed to end in a terrible sigh.

Artos did not turn around. "I believed in the dragon."

Linn did not answer.

"I *loved* the dragon."

The silence behind him was so loud that at last Artos turned around. The old man had fallen onto his side and lay still. Artos felt something warm on his cheeks and realized they were tears. He ran to Linn and knelt down, pulling the old man onto his lap. As he cradled him, Linn opened his eyes.

"Did you bring me any stew?" he asked.

"I . . ." the tears were falling unchecked now. "I brought you seed cakes."

"I like seed cakes," Linn said. "But couldn't you get any stew from Old Garlic?"

Artos felt his mouth drop open. "How did you know about her?"

The old man smiled, showing terrible teeth. He whispered: "I am the Great Riddler. I am the Master of Wisdom. I am the Word and I am the Light. I Was and Am and Will Be." He hesitated. "I am the Dragon."

Artos smiled back and then carefully stood with the old man in his arms. He was amazed at how frail Linn was. His bones, Artos thought, must be as hollow as the wing bones of a bird.

There was a door in the cave wall and Linn signaled him

toward it. Carrying the old apothecary through the doorway, Artos marveled at the runes carved in the lintel. Past the door was a warren of hallways and rooms. From somewhere ahead he heard the chanting of many men.

Artos looked down at the old man and whispered to him. "Yes. I understand. You *are* the dragon, indeed. And I am the dragon's boy. But I will not let you die just yet. I have not finished getting my wisdom."

Smiling broadly, the old man turned toward him like a baby rooting at its mother's breast, found the seed cakes, ate one of them and then, with a gesture both imperious and fond, stuffed the other in Artos' mouth.

So in the greatest church of London (whether it were Paul's or not the French book maketh no mention) all the estates were long or day in the church for to pray. And when matins and the first mass were done, there was seen in the churchyard, against the high altar, a great stone four square, like unto a marble stone; and in midst thereof was like an anvil of steel a foot on high, and therein stuck a fair sword naked by the point, and letters there were written in gold about the sword that saiden thus:—WHOSO PULLETH OUT THIS SWORD OF THIS STONE AND ANVIL, IS RIGHTWISE KING BORN OF ALL ENGLAND.

—Le Morte D'Arthur
by Sir Thomas Malory

The
Sword
and the Stone

"Would you believe a sword in a stone, my liege?" the old necromancer asked. "I dreamed of one last night. Stone white as whey with a sword stuck in the top like a knife through butter. It means something. My dreams always mean something. Do you believe that stone and that sword, my lord?"

The man on the carved wooden throne sighed heavily, his breath causing the hairs of his mustache to flap. "Merlinnus, I have no time to believe in a sword in a stone. Or on a stone. Or under a stone. I'm just too damnably tired for believing today. And you *always* have dreams."

"This dream is different, my liege."

"They're always different. But I've just spent half a morning pacifying two quarreling *dux bellorum*. Or is it *bellori?*"

"*Belli,*" muttered the mage, shaking his head.

"Whatever. And sorting out five counterclaims from my chief cook and his mistresses. He should stick to his kitchen. His affairs are a mess. And awarding grain to a lady whose miller maliciously killed her cat. Did you know, Merlinnus, that we actually have a law about cat killing that levies a fine of the amount of grain that will cover the dead cat completely when it is held up by the tip of its tail and its nose touches the ground? It took over a peck of grain." He sighed again.

"A large cat, my lord," mumbled the mage.

"A *very* large cat indeed," agreed the king, letting his head sink into his hands. "And a *very* large lady. With a lot of *very* large and important lands. Now what in Mithras' name do I want a sword and a stone for when I have to deal with all that?"

"In *Christ's* name, my lord. *Christ's* name. Remember, we are Christians now." The mage held up a gnarled forefinger. "And it is a sword *in* a stone."

"*You* are the Christian," the king said. "*I* still drink bull's blood with my men. It makes them happy, though the taste of it is somewhat less than good claret." He laughed mirthlessly. "And yet I wonder how good a Christian you are, Merlinnus, when you still insist on talking to trees. Oh, there are those who have seen you walking in your wood and talking, always talking, even though there is no one there. Once a Druid, always a Druid, so Sir Kai says."

"Kai is a fool," answered the old man, crossing himself quickly as if marking the points of the body punctuated his thought.

"Kai is a fool, indeed, but even fools have ears and eyes. Go away, Merlinnus, and do not trouble me with this sword on a stone. I have more important things to deal with." He made several dismissing movements with his left hand while summoning the next petitioner with his right. The petitioner, a young woman with a saucy smile and a bodice bouncing with promises, moved forward. The king smiled back.

Merlinnus left and went outside, walking with more care

than absolutely necessary, to the grove beyond the castle walls where his favorite oak grew. He addressed it rather informally, they being of a long acquaintance.

"Salve, amice frondifer, greetings, friend leaf bearer. What am I to do with that boy? When I picked him out it was because the blood of a strong-minded and lusty king ran in his veins, though on the sinister side. Should I then have expected gratitude and imagination to accompany such a heritage? Ah, but unfortunately I did. My brains must be rotting away with age. Tell me, *e glande nate,* sprout of an acorn, do I ask too much? Vision! That's what is missing, is it not?"

A rustle of leaves, as if a tiny wind puzzled through the grove, was his only answer.

Merlinnus sat down at the foot of the tree and rubbed his back against the bark, easing an itch that had been there since breakfast. He tucked the skirt of his woolen robe between his legs and stared at his feet. He still favored the Roman summer sandals, even into late fall, because closed boots tended to make the skin crackle between his toes like old parchment. And besides, in the heavy boots, his feet sweated and stank. But he always felt cold now, winter and summer. So he wore a woolen robe year-round.

"Did I address him incorrectly, do you think? These new kings are such sticklers for etiquette. An old man like me finds that stuff boring. Such a waste of time, and time is the one commodity I have so little of." He rubbed a finger alongside his nose.

"I thought to pique his interest, to get him wondering about a sword that is stuck in a stone like a knife in a slab of fresh beef. A bit of legerdemain, that, and I'm rather proud of it actually. You see, it wasn't *just* a dream. I've done it up in my tower room. Anyone with a bit of knowledge can read the old Latin building manuals and construct a ring of stones. Building the baths under the castle was harder work. But that sword in the stone—yes, I'm rather proud of it. And what that young king has got to realize is that he needs to do something more than rule on cases of quarreling dukes and petty mistresses and grasping rich widows. He has to..." stopping for a minute to listen to the wind again through trees, Merlinnus shook his head and went on. "He has to fire up these silly tribes, give them something magical to rally them. I don't mean him to be just another petty chieftain. Oh, no. He's to be my greatest creation, that boy." He rubbed his nose again. "My last creation, I'm afraid. If this one doesn't work out, what am I to do?"

The wind, now stronger, soughed through the trees.

"I was given just thirty-three years to bind this kingdom, you know. That's the charge, the geas laid on me: thirty-three years to bind it *per crucem et quercum,* by cross and by oak. And this, alas, is the last year."

A cuckoo called down from the limb over his head.

"The first one I tried was that idiot Uther. Why, his head was more wood than thine." The old man chuckled to himself. "And then there were those twins from the Hebrides who enjoyed games so much. Then that witch, Morgana. She made a pretty mess of things. I even considered—at her prompting—her strange, dark little son. Or was he her nephew? I forget which. When one has been a lifelong celibate as I, one tends to dismiss such frequent and casual couplings and their messy aftermaths as unimportant. But that boy had a sly, foxy look about him. Nothing would follow him but a pack of dogs. And then I found this one right under my nose. In some ways he's the dullest of the lot, and yet in a king dullness can be a virtue. *If* the crown is secure."

A nut fell on his head, tumbled down his chest, and landed in his lap. It was a walnut, which was indeed strange since he was sitting beneath an oak. Expecting magic, the mage looked up. There was a little red squirrel staring down at him. Merlinnus cracked the nut between two stones, extracted the meat, and held up half to the squirrel.

"Walnuts from acorn trees," he said. As soon as the squirrel had snatched away its half of the nut meat, the old man drifted off into a dream-filled sleep.

"Wake up, wake up, old one." It was the shaking, not the sentence, that woke him. He opened his eyes. A film of sleep lent a soft focus to his vision. The person standing over him seemed haloed in mist.

"Are you all right, grandfather?" The voice was soft, too.

Merlinnus sat up. He was, he guessed, too old to be sleeping out of doors. The ground cold had seeped into his bones. Like an old tree, his sap ran sluggishly. But being caught out by a youngster made him grumpy. "Why shouldn't I be all right?" he answered, more gruffly than he meant.

"You are so thin, grandfather, and you sleep so silently. I feared you dead. One should not die in a sacred grove. It offends the Goddess."

"Are you then a worshipper of the White One?" he asked, carefully watching the stranger's hands. No true worshipper would answer that question in a straightforward manner, but would instead signal the dark secret with an inconspicuous semaphore. But all that the fingers signed were concern for him. Forefinger, fool's finger, physic's finger, ear finger were silent of secrets. Merlinnus sighed and struggled to sit upright.

The stranger put a hand under his arm and back and gently eased him into a comfortable position. Once up, Merlinnus took a better look. The stranger was a boy with that soft lambent cheek not yet coarsened by a beard. His eyes were the clear blue of speedwells. The eyebrows were dark swallow wings, sweeping high and back toward luxuriant and surprisingly gold hair caught under a dark cap. He was dressed in homespun, but neat and clean. His hands, clasped before him, were small and well formed.

Sensing the mage's inspecton, the boy spoke. "I have come in the hopes of becoming a page at court."

Catamite! Merlinnus thought but did not speak it aloud. The Romans had much to answer for. It was not all roadways and baths.

But, as if anticipating the old man's rising disgust, the boy added, "I wish to learn the sword and lance, and I have sworn myself to purity till I be pledged."

Merlinnus' mouth screwed about a bit but at last settled into a passable smile. Perhaps he could find some use for the boy. A wedge properly placed had been known to split a mighty tree. And he had so little time. "What is your name, boy?"

"I am called . . ." there was a hesitation, scarcely noticeable. "Gawen."

Merlin's smiled broadened. "Ah, but we have already a great knight by a similar name. He is praised as one of the king's Three Fearless Men."

"Fearless in bed, certainly," the boy answered. "The hollow man." Then, as if to soften his words, he added, "Or so it is said where I come from."

So, Merlinnus thought, there may be more to this than a child come to court. Aloud, he said, "And where *do* you come from?"

The boy looked down and smoothed the homespun where it lay against his thighs. "The coast."

Refusing to comment that the coast was many miles long both north and south, Merlinnus said sharply, "Do not condemn a man with another's words. And do not praise him that way, either."

The boy did not answer.

"Purity in tongue must proceed purity in body," the mage added for the boy's silence annoyed him. "That is my first lesson to you."

A small sulky voice answered him. "I am too old for lessons."

"None of us is too old," said Merlinnus, wondering why he felt so compelled to go on and on. Then, as if to soften his criticism, he added, "Even I learned something today."

"And that is . . . ?"

"It has to do with the Matter of Britain," the mage said, "and is therefore beyond you."

"Why beyond me?"

"Give me your hand." He held his own out, crabbed with age.

Gawen reluctantly put his small hand forward, and the mage ran a finger across the palm, slicing the lifeline where it forked early.

"I see you are no stranger to work. The calluses tell me that. But what work it is I do not know."

Gawen withdrew his hand and smiled brightly, his mouth wide, mobile, telling of obvious relief.

Merlinnus wondered what other secrets the hand might have told him could he have read palms as easily as a village herb wife. Then, shaking his head, he stood.

"Come. Before I bring you into court, let us go and wash ourselves in the river."

The boy's eyes brightened. *"You* can bring me to court?"

With more pride than he felt and more hope than he had any right to feel, Merlinnus smiled." Of course, my son. After all, I am the High King's mage."

They walked companionably to the river which ran noisily between stones. Willows on the bank wept their leaves into the swift current. Merlinnus used the willow trunks for support as he sat down carefully on the bank. He eased his feet, sandals and all, into the cold water. It was too far and too slippery for him to stand.

"Bring me enough to bathe with," he said, pointing to the water. It could be a test of the boy's quick-wittedness.

Gawan stripped off his cap, knelt down, and held the cap in the river. Then he pulled it out and wrung the water over the old man's hands.

Merlinnus liked that. The job had been done, and quickly, with little wasted motion. Another boy might have plunged into the river, splashing like an untrained animal. Or asked what to do.

The boy muttered, *"De matri a patre."*

Startled, Merlinnus looked up into the clear, untroubled blue eyes. "You know Latin?"

"Did I . . . did I say it wrong?"

"From the mother to the father."

"That is what I meant." Gawen's young face was immediately transformed by the wide smile. "The . . . the brothers taught me."

Merlinnus knew only two monasteries along the coast and they were very far away. The sisters of Quintern Abbey were much closer, but they never taught boys. This child, thought the mage, has come a very long way indeed. Aloud, he said, "They taught you well."

Gawen bent down again, dipped the cap once more, and this time used the water to wash his own face and hands. Then he wrung the cap out thoroughly, but did not put it back on his head. Cap in hand, he faced the mage. "You *will* bring me to the High King, then?"

A sudden song welled up in Merlinnus' breast, a high hallelujah so unlike any of the dark chantings he was used to under the oaks. "I will," he said.

As they neared the castle, the sun was setting. It was unusually brilliant, rain and fog being the ordinary settings for evenings in early fall. The high tor, rumored to be hollow, was haloed with gold and loomed up behind the topmost towers.

Gawen gasped at the high timbered walls.

Merlinnus smiled to himself but said nothing. For a child from the coast, such walls must seem near miraculous. But for the competent architect who planned for eternity, mathematics was miracle enough. He had long studied the writing of the Roman builders, whose prose styles were as tedious as their knowledge was great. He had learned from them how to instruct men in the slotting of breastwork timbers. All he had needed was the ability to read—and time. Yet time, he thought bitterly, for construction as with everything else had all but run out for him. Still, there was this boy— and this *now*.

"Come," said the mage. "Stand tall and enter."

The boy squared his shoulders, and they hammered upon the carved wooden doors together.

Having first checked them out through the spyhole, the guards opened the doors with a desultory air that marked them at the end of their watch.

"*Ave*, Merlinnus," said one guard with an execrable accent. It was obvious he knew that much Latin and no more. The other guard was silent.

Gawen was silent as well, but his small silence was filled with wonder. Merlinnus glanced slantwise and saw the boy taking in the great stoneworks, the Roman mosaic panel on the entry wall, all the fine details he had insisted upon. He remembered the argument with Morgana when they had built that wall.

"An awed emissary," he had told her, "is already half won over."

At least she had had the wit to agree, though later those same wits had been addled by drugs and wine and the gods only knew what other excesses. Merlinnus shook his head.

It was best to look forward not back when you have so little time. Looking backward was an old man's drug.

He put his hand on the boy's shoulder, feeling the fine bones beneath the jerkin. "Turn here," he said softly.

They turned into the long, dark walkway where the walls were niched for the slide of three separate portcullises. No invaders could break in this way. Merlinnus was proud of the castle's defenses.

As they walked, Gawen's head was constantly aswivel: left, right, up, down. Wherever he had come from had left him unprepared for this. At last the hall opened into an inner courtyard where pigs, poultry, and wagons vied for space.

Gawen breathed out again. "It's like home," he whispered.

"Eh?" Merlinnus let out a whistle of air like a skin bag deflating.

"Only finer, of course." The quick answer almost satisfying, but not quite. Not quite. And Merlinnus was not one to enjoy unsolved puzzles.

"To the right," the old man growled, shoving his finger hard into the boy's back. "To the right."

They were ushered into the throne room without a moment's hesitation. This much, at least, a long memory and a reputation for magic making and king making brought him.

The king looked up from the paper he was laboriously reading, his finger marking his place. He always, Merlinnus noted with regret, read well behind that finger for he had come to reading as a grown man, and reluctantly, his fingers faster in all activities than his mind. But he *was* well-meaning, the mage reminded himself. Just a bit sluggish on the uptake. A king should be faster than his advisors, though he seem to lean upon them; quicker than his knights, though he seem to send them on ahead.

"Ah, Merlinnus, I am glad you are back. There's a dinner tonight with an emissary from the Orkneys and you know I have trouble understanding their rough mangling of English. You will be there?"

Merlinnus nodded.

"And there is a contest I need your advice on. Here." He snapped his fingers and a list was put into his hand.

"The men want to choose a May queen to serve next year. I think they are hoping to thrust her on me as my queen. They have drawn up a list of those qualities they think she should possess. Kai wrote the list down."

Kai, Merlinnus thought disagreeably, was the only one of that crew who *could* write and his spelling was only marginally better than his script. He took the list and scanned it:

> *Thre things smalle—headde, nose, breestes;*
> *Thre things largge—waiste, hippes, calves;*
> *Thre thingges longge—haires, finggers, thies;*
> *Thre thingges short—height, toes, utterance.*

"Sounds more like an animal in a bestiary than a girl, my lord," Merlinnus ventured at last.

Gawen giggled.

"They are trying—" the king began.

"They certainly are," muttered the mage.

"They are trying . . . to be helpful, Merlinnus." The king glowered at the boy by the mage's side. "And who is this fey bit of work?"

The boy bowed deeply. "I am called Gawen, sire, and I have come to learn to be a knight."

The king ground his teeth. "And some of them, no doubt, will like you be-nights."

A flush spread across the boy's cheeks. "I am sworn to the Holy Mother to be pure," he said.

"Are you a grailer or a Goddess worshipper?" Before the boy could answer, the king turned to Merlinnus. "Is he well bred?"

"Of course," said Merlinnus, guessing. The Latin and the elegant speech said as much, even without the slip about how much a castle looked like home.

"Very well," the king said, arching his back and putting one hand behind him. "Damned throne's too hard. I think I actually prefer a soldier's pallet. Or a horse." He stood and stretched. "That's enough for one day. I will look at the rest tomorrow." He put out a hand and steadied himself, using the mage's shoulder, then descended the two steps to the ground. Whispering in Merlinnus' right ear because he knew the left ear was a bit deafened by age, the king said, "When you gave me the kingdom, you forgot to mention that kings need to sit all day long. You neglected to tell me about wooden thrones. If you had told me that when you offered me the crown, I might have thought about it a bit longer."

"And would you have made a different choice, my lord?" asked Merlinnus quietly.

The king laughed and said aloud, "No, but I would have requested a different throne."

Merlinnus looked shocked. "But that is the High King's throne. Without it, you would not be recognized."

The king nodded.

Gawen, silent until this moment, spoke up. "Would not a cushion atop the throne do? Like the crown atop the High King's head?"

The king's hand went immediately to the heavy circlet of metal on his head. Then he swept it off, shook out his long blonde locks, and laughed. "Of course. A cushion. Out of the mouth of babes . . . it would do, would it not, Merlinnus?"

The mage's mouth twisted about the word. "Cushion." But he could think of no objection. It was the quiet homeyness of the solution that offended him. But certainly it would work.

Merlinnus put aside his niggling doubts about the boy Gawen and turned instead to the problem at hand: making the king accept the magic of the sword in the stone.

"I beg you, sire," the old mage said the next morning, "to listen." He accompanied his request with a bow on bended knee. The pains of increasing age were only slightly mitigated by some tisanes brewed by a local herb wife. Merlinnus sighed heavily as he went down. It was that sigh, sounding so much like his old grandfather's, that decided the king.

"All right, all right, Merlinnus. Let us see this sword and this stone."

"It is in my workroom," Merlinnus said. "If you will accompany me there." He tried to stand and could not.

"I will not only accompany you," said the king patiently,

"it looks as if I will have to carry you." He came down from his throne and lifted the old man up to his feet.

"I can walk," Merlinnus said, somewhat testily.

Arm in arm, they wound through the castle halls, up three flights of stone stairs to Merlinnus' tower workroom.

The door opened with a spoken spell and three keys. The king seemed little impressed.

"There!" said the mage, pointing to a block of white marble with veins of red and green running through. Sticking out of the stone top was the hilt of a sword. The hilt was carved with wonderful runes. On the white marble face was the legend:

> WHOSO PULLETH OUTE THIS SWERD OF THIS STONE
> IS RIGHTWYS KYNGE BORNE OF
> ALL BRYTAYGNE

Slowly the king read aloud, his finger tracing the letters in the stone. When he had finished, he looked up. "But *I* am king of all Britain."

"Then pull the sword, sire."

The king smiled and it was not a pleasant smile. He was a strong man, in his prime, and except for his best friend Sir Lancelot, was reputed to be the strongest in the kingdom. It was one of the reasons Merlinnus had chosen him. He put his hand to the hilt, tightened his fingers around it until the knuckles were white, and pulled.

The sword remained in the stone.

"Merlinnus, this is witchery. I will not have it." His voice was cold.

"And with *witchery* you will pull it out in full view of the admiring throngs. You—and no one else." The mage smiled benignly.

The king let go of the sword. "But why this? I am *already* king."

"Because I hear grumblings in the kingdom. Oh, do not look slantwise at me, boy. It is not magic but reliable spies that tell me so. There are those who refuse to follow you, to be bound to you and so bind this kingdom because they doubt the legitimacy of your claim."

The king snorted. "And they are right, Merlinnus. I am

king because the arch-mage wills it. *Per crucem et quer-cum.*"

Startled, Merlinnus asked, "How did you know that?"

"Oh, my old friend, do you think you are the only one with reliable spies?"

Merlinnus stared into the king's eyes. "Yes, you are right. You are king because I willed it. And because you earned it. But this bit of legerdemain . . ."

"Witchery!" interrupted the king.

Merlinnus persisted. "This *legerdemain* will have them all believing in you." He added quickly, "As I do. *All* of them. To bind the kingdom you need *all* the tribes to follow you."

The king looked down and then, as if free of the magic for a moment, turned and stared out of the tower window to the north where winter was already creeping down the mountainsides. "Do those few tribes matter? The ones who paint themselves blue and squat naked around small fires. The ones who wrap themselves in woolen blankets and blow noisily into animal bladders calling it song? The ones who dig out shelled fish with their toes and eat the fish raw? Do we really want to bring them to our kingdom?"

"They are all part of Britain. The Britain of which you are the king now and for the future."

The king shifted his gaze from the mountains to the guards walking his donjon walls. "Are you positive I shall be able to draw the sword? I will *not* be made a mockery to satisfy some hidden purpose of yours."

"Put your hand on the sword, sire."

The king turned slowly as if the words had a power to command him. He walked back to the marble. It seemed to glow. He reached out and then, before his hand touched the hilt, by an incredible act of will, he stopped. "I am a good soldier, Merlinnus. And I love this land."

"I know."

With a resonant slap the king's hand grasped the sword. Merlinnus muttered something in a voice as soft as a cradle song. The sword slid noiselessly from the stone.

Holding the sword above his head, the king turned and looked steadily at the mage. "If I were a wicked man, I would bring this down on your head. Now."

"I know."

Slowly the sword descended and, when it was level with his eyes, the king put his left hand to the hilt as well. He hefted the sword several times and made soft comfortable noises deep in his chest. Then, carefully, like a woman threading a needle, he slid the sword back into its slot in the stone.

"I will have my men take this and place it before the great cathedral so that all might see it. *All* my people shall have a chance to try their hands."

"All?"

"Even the ones who paint themselves blue or blow into bladders or do other disgusting and uncivilized things." The king smiled. "I shall even let mages try."

Merlinnus smiled back. "Is that wise?"

"I am the one with the strong arm, Merlinnus. You are to provide the wisdom. And the witchery."

"Then let the mages try, too," Merlinnus said. "For all the good it will do them."

"It is a fine sword, Merlinnus. It shall honor its wielder." He put his hand back on the hilt and heaved. The sword did not move.

The soldiers, with no help from Merlinnus, moaned and pushed and sweated and pulled until at last they managed to remove the sword and stone with a series of rollers and ropes. At the king's request it was set up in front of the great cathedral in the center of the town outside the castle walls. News of it was carried by carters and jongleurs, gleemen and criers from castle to castle and town to town. Within a month the hilt of the sword was filthy from the press of hundreds of hands. It seemed that in the countryside there were many who would be king.

Young Gawen took it upon himself to clean the hilt whenever he had time. He polished the runes on the stone lovingly, too, and studied the white marble from all angles. But he never put his hand to the sword as if to pull it. When the king was told of this, he smiled and his hand strayed to the cushion beneath him.

Gawen reported on the crowds around the stone to Merlinnus as he recounted his other lessons.

"Helm, aventail, byrnie, gauntlet, cuisses..." he re-
cited, touching the parts of his body where the armor would
rest. "And arch-mage, there was a giant of a man there
today, dressed all in black, who tried the sword. And six
strange tribesmen with blue skin and necklaces of shells.
Two of them tried to pull together. The sword would not
come out, but their blue dye came off. I had a horrible time
scrubbing it from the hilt. And Sir Kai came."

"Again?"

The boy laughed. "It was his sixth try. He waits until it
is dinner time and no one is in the square."

The old mage nodded at every word. "Tell me again."

"About Sir Kai?"

"About the parts of the armor. You must have the lesson
perfect for tomorrow."

The boy's mouth narrowed as he began. "Helm, aventail..."

At each word, Merlinnus felt a surge of pride and puz-
zlement. Though the recitation was an old one, it sounded
new and somehow different in Gawen's mouth.

They waited until the night of the solstice, when the earth
sat posed between night and night. Great bonfires were lit
in front of the cathedral to drive back the darkness, while
inside candles were lighted to do the same.

"It is time," Merlinnus said to the king without any pre-
liminaries.

"It is always time," answered the king, placing his careful
marks on the bottom of yet another piece of parchment.

"I mean time to pull the sword from the stone." Merlinnus
offered his hand to the king.

Pushing aside the offer, the king rose.

"I see you use the cushion now," Merlinnus said.

"It helps somewhat." He stretched. "I only wish I had
two of them."

The mage shook his head. "You are the king. Command
the second."

The king looked at him steadily. "I doubt such excess is
wise."

Remembering Morgana, the mage smiled.

* * *

They walked arm in arm to the waiting horses. Merlinnus was helped onto a gray whose broad back was more like a chair than a charger. But then, he had always been ill at ease on horseback. And horses, even the ones with the calmest dispositions, sensed some strangeness in him. They always shied.

The king strode to his own horse, a barrel-chested bay with a smallish head. It had been his mount when he was a simple soldier and he had resisted all attempts to make him ride another.

"Mount up," the king called to his guards.

Behind him his retinue mounted. Sir Kai was the first to vault into the saddle. Young Gawen, astride the pony that was a present from the king, was the last.

With a minimum of fuss, they wound along the path down the hillside toward the town, and only the clopping of hooves on dirt marked their passage. Ahead were torch-bearers and behind them came the household, each with a candle. So light came to light, a wavering parade to the waiting stone below.

In the fire-broken night the white stone gleamed before the black hulk of the cathedral. The darker veins in the stone meandered like faery streams across its surface. The sword, now shadow, now light, was the focus of hundreds of eyes. And, as if pulled by some invisible string, the king rode directly to the stone, dismounted, and knelt before it. Then he removed his circlet of office and shook free the long golden mane it had held so firmly in place. When he stood again, he put the crown on the top of the stone so that it lay just below the angled sword.

The crowd fell still.

"This crown and this land belong to the man who can pull the sword from the stone," the king said, his voice booming into the strange silence. "So it is written—here." He gestured broadly with his hand toward the runes.

"Read it," cried a woman's voice from the crowd.

"We want to hear it," shouted another.

A man's voice, picking up her argument, dared a further step. "We want the mage to read it." Anonymity lent his words power. The crowd muttered its agreement.

Merlinnus dismounted carefully and, after adjusting his robes, walked to the stone. He glanced only briefly at the words on its side, then turned to face the people.

"The message on the stone is burned here," he said, pointing to his breast, "here in my heart. It says: *Whoso pulleth out this sword of this stone is rightwise king born of all Britain.*"

Sir Kai nodded and said loudly, "Yes, that is what it says. Right."

The king put his hands on his hips. "And so, good people, the challenge has been thrown down before us all. He who would be king of all Britain must step forward and put his hand on the sword."

At first there was no sound at all but the dying echo of the king's voice. Then a child cried and that started the crowd. They began talking to one another, jostling, arguing, some good-naturedly and others with a belligerent tone. Finally, a rather sheepish farm boy, taller by almost a head than Sir Kai who was the tallest of the knights, was thrust from the crowd. He had a shock of wheat-colored hair over one eye and a dimple in his chin.

"I'd try, my lord," he said. He was plainly uncomfortable having to talk to the king. "I mean, it wouldn't do no harm."

"No harm indeed, son," said the king. He took the boy by the elbow and escorted him to the stone.

The boy put both his hands around the hilt and then stopped. He looked over his shoulder at the crowd. Someone shouted encouragement and then the whole push of people began to call out to him.

"Do it. Pull the bastard. Give it a heave. Haul it out." Their cries came thick now and, buoyed by their excitement, the boy put his right foot up against the stone. Then he leaned backward and pulled. His hands slipped along the hilt and he fell onto his bottom to the delight of the crowd.

Crestfallen, the boy stood up. He stared unhappily at his worn boots as if he did not know where else to look or how to make his feet carry him away.

The king put his hand on the boy's shoulder. "What is your name, son?" The gentleness in his voice silenced the crowd's laughter.

"Percy, sir," the boy managed at last.

"Then, Percy," said the king, "because you were brave enough to try where no one else would set hand on the sword, you shall come to the castle and learn to be one of my knights."

"Maybe not *your* knight," someone shouted from the crowd.

A shadow passed over the king's face and he turned toward the mage.

Merlinnus shook his head imperceptibly and put his finger to his lips.

The king shifted his gaze back to the crowd. He smiled. "No, perhaps not. We shall see. Who else would try?"

At last Sir Kai brushed his hand across his breastplate. He alone of the court still affected the Roman style. Tugging his gloves down so that the fingers fitted snugly, he walked to the stone and placed his right hand on the hilt. He gave it a slight tug, smoothed his golden mustache with the fingers of his left hand, then reached over with his left hand and with both gave a mighty yank. The sword did not move.

Kai shrugged and turned toward the king. "But I am still first in your service," he said.

"And in my heart, brother," acknowledged the king.

Then, one by one, the knights lined up and took turns pulling on the sword. Stocky Bedevere, handsome Gawain, Tristan maned like a lion, cocky Galahad, and the rest. But the sword, ever firm in its stone scabbard, never moved.

At last, of all the court's knights, only Lancelot was left.

"And you, good Lance, my right hand, the strongest of us all, will you not try?" asked the king.

Lancelot, who disdained armor except in battle and was dressed in a simple tunic, the kind one might dance in, shook his head. "I have no wish to be king. I only wish to be of service."

The king walked over to him and put his hand on Lancelot's shoulder. He whispered into the knight's ear. "It is the stone's desire, not ours, that will decide this. But if you do *not* try, then my leadership will always be in doubt. Without your full commitment to this cause, the kingdom will not be bound."

"Then I will put my hand to it, my lord," Lancelot said. "Because you require it, not because I desire it." He shuttered his eyes.

"Do not just put your hand there. You must *try*, damn you," the king whispered fiercely. "You must really try."

Lancelot opened his eyes and some small fire, reflecting perhaps from the candles or the torches or the solstice flames, seemed to glow there for a moment. Then, in an instant, the fire in his eyes was gone. He stepped up to the stone, put his hand to the sword, and seemed to address it. His lips moved but no sound came out. Taking a deep breath, he pulled. Then, letting the breath out slowly, he leaned back.

The stone began to move.

The crowd gasped in a single voice.

"*Arthur . . .*" Kai began, his hand on the king's arm.

Sweat appeared on Lancelot's brow and the king could feel an answering band of sweat on his own. He could feel the weight of Lancelot's pull between his own shoulder blades and he held his breath with the knight.

The stone began to slide along the courtyard mosaic, but the sword did not slip from its mooring. It was a handle for the stone, nothing more. After a few inches, the stone stopped moving. Lancelot withdrew his hand from the hilt, bowed slightly toward the king, and took two steps back.

"I cannot unsheath the king's sword," he said. His voice was remarkably level for a man who had just moved a ton of stone.

"Is there no one else?" asked Merlinnus, slowly looking around.

No one in the crowd dared to meet his eyes and there followed a long, full silence.

Then, from the left, came a familiar light voice. "Let King Arthur try." It was Gawen.

At once the crowd picked up its cue. "Arthur! Arthur! Arthur!" they shouted. And, wading into their noise like a swimmer in heavy swells breasting the waves, the king walked to the stone. Putting his right hand on the sword hilt, he turned his face to the people.

"For Britain!" he cried.

Merlinnus nodded, crossed his forefingers, and sighed a spell in Latin.

Arthur pulled. With a slight *whoosh* the sword slid out of the slot. He put his left hand above his right on the hilt and swung the sword over his head once, twice, and then a third time. Then he brought it slowly down before him until its point touched the earth.

"Now I be king. Of *all* Britain," he said.

Kai picked up the circlet from the stone and placed it on Arthur's head, and the chant of his name began anew. But even as he was swept up, up, up into the air by Kai and Lancelot to ride their shoulders above the crowd, Arthur's eyes met the mage's. He whispered fiercely to Merlinnus who could read his lips though his voice could scarcely carry against the noise.

"I will see you in your tower. Tonight!"

Merlinnus was waiting when two hours later the king slipped into his room, the sword in his left hand.

"So now you are king of all Britain indeed," said Merlinnus. "And none can say you no. Was I not right? A bit of legerdemain and . . ."

The king's face was gray in the room's candlelight. "Merlinnus, you do not understand. I am *not* the king. There is another."

"Another what?" asked the mage.

"Another king. Another sword."

Merlinnus shook his head. "You are tired, lord. It has been a long day and an even longer night."

Arthur came over and grabbed the old man's shoulder with his right hand. "Merlinnus, *this is not the same sword.*"

"My lord, you are mistaken. It can be no other."

Arthur swept the small crown off his head and dropped it into the mage's lap. "I am a simple man, Merlinnus, and I am an honest one. I do not know much, though I am trying to learn more. I read slowly and understand only with help. What I am best at is soldiering. What I know best is swords. The sword I held months ago in my hands is not the sword I hold now. That sword had a balance to it, a grace such as

I had never felt before. It knew me, knew my hand. There was a pattern on the blade that looked now like wind, now like fire. This blade, though it has fine watering, looks like nothing.

"I am not an imaginative man, Merlinnus, so I am not imagining this. This is not the sword that was in the stone. And if it is not, where is that sword? And what man took it? For he, not I, is the rightful born king of all Britain. And I would be the first in the land to bend my knee to him."

Merlinnus put his hand to his head and stared at the crown in his lap. "I swear to you, Arthur, no man alive could move that sword from the stone lest I spoke the words."

There was a slight sound from behind the heavy curtains bordering the window, and a small figure emerged holding a sword in two hands. "I am afraid that I took the sword, my lords."

"Gawen!" cried Merlinnus and Arthur at once.

The boy knelt before Arthur and held up the sword before him.

Arthur bent down and pulled the boy up. The sword was between them.

"It is I should kneel to you, my young king."

Gawen shook his head and a slight flush covered his cheeks. "I cannot be king now or ever. Not *rex quondam, rexque futurus.*"

"How pulled you the sword, then?" Merlinnus asked. "Speak. Be quick about it."

The boy placed the sword in Arthur's hands. "I brought a slab of butter to the stone one night and melted the butter over candle flames. When it was a river of gold I poured it into the slot and the sword slid out. Just like that."

"A trick. A homey trick that any herb wife might . . ." Merlinnus began.

Arthur turned on him, sadly. "No more a trick, mage, than my pulling a sword loosed by your spell. The boy is, in fact, the better of us two, for he worked it out by himself." He shifted and spoke directly to Gawen. "A king needs such cunning. But he needs a good right hand as well. I shall be yours, my lord, though I envy you the sword."

"The sword is yours, Arthur, never mine. Though I can

now thrust and slash, having learned that much under the ham-handedness of your good tutor, I shall not ride to war. I have learned to fear the blade's edge as well as respect it." Gawen smiled.

The king turned again to Merlinnus. "Help me, mage. I do not understand."

Merlinnus rose and put the crown back on Arthur's head. "But I think I do, at last, though why I should be so slow to note it, I wonder. Age must dull the mind as well as the fingers. I have had an ague of the brain this fall. I said no man but you could pull the sword—and no *man* has." He held out his hand. "Come, child. You shall make a lovely May queen, I think. By then the hair should be long enough for Sir Kai's list, though what, I think, we shall ever do about the short utterances is beyond me."

"A *girl?* He's a girl?" Arthur looked baffled.

"Magic even beyond my making," said Merlinnus. "But what is your name, child? Surely not Gawen."

"Guenevere," she said. "I came to learn to be a knight in order to challenge Sir Gawain who had dishonored my sister. But I find—"

"That he is a bubblehead and not worth the effort?" interrupted Arthur. "He shall marry her *and* he shall be glad of it, for you shall be my queen and, married to your sister, he shall be my brother."

Guenevere laughed. "She will like that, too. Her head is as empty as his. But she *is* my sister. And without a brother to champion her, I had to do."

Merlinnus laughed. "And you did splendidly. But about that butter trick . . ."

Guenevere put her hand over her breast. "I shall never tell as long as . . ." she hesitated.

"Anything," Arthur said. "Ask for anything."

"As long as I can have my sword back."

Arthur looked longingly at the sword, hefted it once, and then put it solemnly in her hand.

"Oh, not *this* one," Guenevere said. "It is too heavy and unwieldy. It does not sit well in my hand. I mean the other, the one you pulled."

"Oh, *that,*" said Arthur. "With all my heart."

This is what Merlin advised: to go to Ireland to the place called the Giants' Circle on Mount Killara, for there were stones of a marvellous appearance. "And there is no one, lord, in this age who knows anything about those stones. And they shall not be got by might or by strength, but by art. And if these stones were here as they are there, they would stand forever."

—Historia Regum Britanniae
by Geoffrey of Monmouth

Merlin at Stonehenge

How could you know, seeing it today,
Stones upon stones, lintel and base,
The hallowing it set in play
For that long forgotten race
Who worshipped and who danced below
The hanging stones—how could you know?

How could you know, a traveler here
To view the sight through camera lens,
How this great rock dance did appear?

You get your shot, you pay your pence,
Then briefly glance around the place,
This mummery of a long lost race.

You see but stones, I saw a king,
A place, a time where time was not,
A sword and crown foreshadowing
The world without a Camelot.
The image fades but does not die,
And no one knows so well as I.

You see but circles, I saw stars;
A horseshoe where I counted sun
And the slow encircling Mars
That crowned the stones when day was done
And sounded out the deep refrain
Of faith upon Salisbury Plain.

Was it strange men in hot parade
Who set the stones upon the grass
Then picnicked in the lengthening shade
And watched the English noontide pass?
Or was it magic by some mage
Who did these very stones engage?

The tale's been told. I am not shy
To claim the credit for this ring.
All stories do not have to lie,
All lying's not an evil thing.
I piped the stones off Erin's land.
The mouth is mightier than the hand.

This be sage handiwork, I swear,
Hic jacet Merlinnus Magister.

And as they rode, Arthur said, "I have no sword."

"No force," said Merlin, "hereby is a sword that shall be yours, an I may."

So they rode till they came to a lake, the which was a fair water and broad, and in the midst of the lake Arthur was ware of an arm clothed in white samite, that held a fair sword in that hand.

"Lo!" said Merlin, "yonder is that sword that I spake of."

With that they saw a damosel going upon the lake.

"What damosel is that?" said Arthur.

"That is the Lady of the Lake," said Merlin; "and within that lake is a rock, and therein is as fair a place as any on earth, and richly beseen; and this damosel will come to you anon, and then speak ye fair to her that she will give you that sword."

—Le Morte D'Arthur
by Sir Thomas Malory

Evian
Steel

Ynis Evelonia, the Isle of Women, lies within the marshy tidal river Tamor that is itself but a ribbon stretched between the Mendip and the Quantock hills. The isle is scarcely remarked from the shore. It is as if Manannan MacLir himself had shaken his cloak between.·

On most days there is an unsettling mist obscuring the irregular coast of the isle; and only in the full sun, when the light just rising illuminates a channel, can any passage across the glass-colored waters be seen. And so it is that women alone, who have been schooled in the hidden cause-ways across the fen, mother to daughter down through the

*years, can traverse the river in coracles that slip easily
through the brackish flood.*

*By ones and twos they come and go in their light skin
boats to commerce with the Daughters of Eve who stay in
holy sistership on the isle, living out their chaste lives and
making with their magicks the finest blades mankind has
ever known.*

*The isle is dotted with trees, not the great Druidic oaks
that line the roadways into Godney and Meare and tower
over the mazed pathways up to the high tor, but small
womanish trees: alder and apple, willow and ash, leafy
havens for the migratory birds. And the little isle fair rings
with bird song and the clanging of hammer on anvil and
steel.*

*But men who come to buy swords at Ynis Evelonia are
never allowed farther inland than the wattle guest house
with its oratory of wicker wands winded and twisted together
under a rush roof. Only one man has ever slept there and
is—in fact—sleeping there still. But that is the end of this
story—which shall not be told—and the beginning of yet
another.*

Elaine stared out across the gray waters as the ferret-
faced woman rowed them to the isle. Her father sat unmoving next to her in the prow of the little boat, his hands
clasped together, his jaw tight. His only admonition so far
had been, "Be strong. The daughter of a vavasour does not
cry."

She had not cried, though surely life among the magic
women on Ynis Evelonia would be far different from life
in the draughty but familiar castle at Escalot. At home
women were cosseted but no one feared them as they feared
the Daughters of Eve, unless one had a sharp tongue like
the ostler's wife or Nanny Bess.

Elaine bent over the rim of the hide boat and tried to see
her reflection in the water, the fair skin and the black hair
plaited with such loving care by Nanny Bess that morning.
But all she could make out was a shadow boat skimming
across the waves. She popped one of her braids into her
mouth, remembering Nanny's repeated warning that some
day the braid would grow there: "And what knight would

wed a girl with hair agrowin' in 'er mouth, I asks ye?"
Elaine could hear Nanny's voice, now sharp as a blade,
now quiet as a lullay, whispering in her ear. She sighed.

At the sound her father looked over at her. His eyes, the
faded blue of a late autumn sky, were pained and lines like
runes ran across his brow.

Elaine let the braid drop from her mouth and smiled
tentatively; she could not bear to disappoint him. At her
small attempt at a smile he smiled back and patted her knee.

The wind spit river water into her face, as salty as tears,
and Elaine hurriedly wiped her cheeks with the hem of her
cape. By the time the boat rocked against the shore her face
was dry.

The ferret-faced woman leaped over the side of the coracle and pulled it farther onto the sand so that Elaine and
her father could debark without wading in the muddy tide.
When they looked up, two women in gray robes had appeared to greet them.

"I am Mother Lisanor," said the tallest one to the vavasour. "You must be Bernard of Escalot."

He bowed his head, quickly removing his hat.

"And this," said the second woman, taking Elaine by the
hand, "must be the fair Elaine. Come child. You shall eat
with me and share my bed this night. A warm body shall
keep away any bad dreams."

"Madam..." the vavasour began.

"*Mother* Sonda," the woman interrupted him.

"Mother Sonda, may my daughter and I have a moment
to say good-bye? She has never been away from home
before." There was the slightest suggestion of a break in
his voice.

"We have found, Sir Bernard, that it is best to part quickly.
I *had* suggested in my letter to you that you leave Elaine
on the Shapwick shore. This is an island of women. Men
come here for commerce sake alone. Ynis Evelonia is Elaine's
home now. But fear you not. We shall train her well." She
gave a small tug on Elaine's hand and started up the hill
and Elaine, all unprotesting, went with her.

Only once, at the top of the small rise, did Elaine turn
back. Her father was still standing by the coracle, hat in
hand, the sun setting behind him. He was haloed against

the darkening sky. Elaine made a small noise, almost a whimper. Then she popped the braid in her mouth. Like a cork in a bottle, it stoppered the sound. Without a word more, she followed Mother Sonda toward the great stone house that nestled down in the valley in the very center of the isle.

The room in the smithy was lit only by the flickering of the fire as Mother Hesta pumped the bellows with her foot. A big woman, whose right arm was more muscular than her left, Hesta seemed comfortable with tools rather than with words. The air from the bellows blew up a sudden large flame that had a bright blue heart.

"See, there. *There*. When the flames be as long as an arrow and the heart of the arrowhead be blue, thrust the blade in," she said, speaking to the new apprentice.

Elaine shifted from one foot to another, rubbing the upper part of her right arm where the brand of Eve still itched. Then she twisted one of her braids up and into her mouth, sucking on the end while she watched but saying nothing.

"You'll see me do this again and again, girl," the forge mistress said. "But it be a year afore I let you try it on your own. For now, you must watch and listen and learn. Fire and water and air make Evian steel, fire and water and air. They be three of the four majorities. And one last thing— though I'll not tell you that yet, for that be our dearest secret. But harken: what be made by the Daughters of Eve strikes true. All men know this and that be why they come here, crost the waters, for our blades. They come, hating it that they must, but knowing only at our forge on this holy isle can they buy this steel. It be the steel that cuts through evil, that strikes the heart of what it seeks."

The girl nodded and her attention blew upon the small fire of words.

"It matters not, child, that we make a short single edge, or what the old Romies called a *glady-us*. It matters not we make a long blade or a double edge. If it be Evian steel, it strikes true." She brought the side of her hand down in a swift movement which made the girl blink twice, but otherwise she did not move, the braid still in her mouth.

Mother Hesta turned her back on the child and returned

to work, the longest lecture done. Her muscles under the short sleeved tunic bunched and flattened. Sweat ran over her arms like an exotic chain of water beads as she hammered steadily on the sword, flattening, shaping, beating out the swellings and bulges that only *her* eye could see, only her fingers could find. The right arm beat, the left arm, with its fine traceries of scars, held.

After a while, the girl's eyes began to blink with weariness and with the constant probings of the irritating smoke. She dropped the braid and it lay against her linen shirt limply, leaving a slight wet stain. She rubbed both eyes with her hands but she was careful not to complain.

Mother Hesta did not seem to notice, but she let the fire die down a bit and laid the partially finished sword on the stone firewall. Wiping her grimed hands on her leather apron, she turned to the girl.

"I'm fair famished, I am. Let's go out to garden where Mother Sonda's set us a meal."

She did not put her hand out to the girl as she was, herself, uncomfortable with such open displays. It was a timeworn joke on Evelonia that Hesta put all her love into pounding at the forge. But she was pleased when the girl trotted by her side without any noticeable hesitation or delay. *A slow apprentice is no apprentice*, Mother Hesta often remarked.

When they stepped out of the shed, the day burst upon them with noisy celebration. Hesta, who spent almost the entire day everyday in her dark forge, was always pleased for a few moments of birds and the colorful assault of the green landscape drifting off into the marshy river beyond. But she was always just as happy to go back into the dark fireroom where the tools slipped comfortably to hand and she could control the *whoosh-whoosh* sigh of the bellows and the loud clangorous song of metal on metal.

A plain cloth was spread upon the grass and a variety of plates covered with napkins awaited them. A jug of watered wine—Hesta hated the feeling heavy wines made in her head when she was working over the hot fire—and two stoneware goblets completed the picture.

"Come," Mother Hesta said.

The word seemed to release the child and she skipped

over to the cloth and squatted down, but she touched nothing on the plate until Hesta had lowered herself to the ground and picked up the first napkin. Then the girl took up a slice of apple and jammed it into her mouth.

Only then did Hesta remember that it was mid-afternoon and the child, who had arrived late the evening before and slept comforted in Mother Sonda's bed, had not eaten since rising. Still, it would not do to apologize. That would make discipline harder. This particular girl, she knew, was the daughter of a vavasour, a man of some means in Escalot. She was not used to serving but to being served, so she must not be coddled now. Hesta was gentle in her chiding, but firm.

"The food'll not disappear, child," she said. "Slow and steady in these things. A buyer for the steel comes to guest house table and he be judging us and we he by what goes on there. A greedy man be a man who'll pay twice what a blade be worth. Discipline, discipline in all things."

The girl, trying to eat more slowly, began to choke.

Hesta poured the goblets halfway full and solemnly handed one to her. The child sipped down her wine and the choking fit ended suddenly. Hesta made no reference to the incident.

"When you be done, collect these plates and cups and take them to yon water house. Mother Argente will meet you there and read you the first chapter of the *Book of Brightness*. Listen well. The ears be daughters of the memory."

"I can read, Mother Hesta," the girl said in a quiet little voice. It was not a boast but information.

"Can you? Then on the morrow you can read to me from the chapter on fire." She did not mention that she, herself a daughter of a landless vassal, had never learned to read. However one came to the *Book*—by eye or ear—did not matter a whit. Some were readers and some were read-tos; each valued in the Goddess' sight, as Argente had promised her many years ago when they had been girls. So she comforted herself still.

"Yes, mother," the girl said. Her voice, though quiet, was unusually low and throaty for one her age. It was a voice that would wear well in the forge room. The last novice had had a whiny voice; she had not remained on the

isle for long. But this girl, big eyed, deep voiced, with a
face the shape of a heart under a waterfall of dark hair, was
such a lovely little thing, she would probably be taken by
the mothers of guest house, Sonda, Lisanor and Katwyn,
no matter how fair her forging. Sometimes, Hesta thought,
the Goddess be hard.

As she watched the girl eating, then wiping her mouth
on the linen square with an easy familiarity, Hesta remembered how mortifying it had been to have to be taught not
to use her sleeve for that duty. Then she smiled because
that memory recalled another, that of a large, rawboned,
parentless ten-year-old-girl she had been, plunging into the
cold channel of the Tamor just moments ahead of the baron
who had claimed her body as his property. He had had to
let her go, exploding powerful curses at her back, for he
could not himself swim. He had been certain that she would
sink. But her body's desperate strength and her crazed de-
termination had brought her safely across the brackish tide
to the isle where, even in a boat, that powerful baron had
not dared go, so fearful was he of the rumors of magic.
And the girl, as much water in as without, had been picked
up out of the rushes by the late forge mistress and laughingly
called Moses after an old tale. And never gone back across
the Tamor, not once these forty years.

In the middle of Hesta's musing, the girl stood up and
began to clear away the dishes to the accompaniment of a
trilling song sung by a modest little brown bird whose flute-
like tunes came daily in spring from the apple bough. It
seemed an omen. Hesta decided she would suggest it to
Mother Sonda as the bird name for the vavasour's child—
Thrush.

There were three other girls in the sleep room when
Elaine was left there. Two of the girls were smoothing their
beds and one was sitting under a corbeled window, staring
out.

Elaine had the braid in her mouth again. Her wide gray
eyes took in everything. Five beds stood in a row along the
wall with wooden chests for linen and other possessions at
each bed foot. A fine Eastern tapestry hung above the beds,
its subject the Daughters of Eve. It depicted about thirty

women at work on a large island surrounded by troubled waves. Against the opposite wall were five arched windows that looked out across the now placid Tamor. Beneath the windows stood two high-warp looms with rather primitive weavings begun on each.

One of the standing girls, a tall wraithy lass with hair the insubstantial color of mist, noticed that Elaine's eyes had taken in the looms.

"We have been learning to weave. It is something that Mother A learned from a traveler in Eastern lands. Not just the simple cloths the peasants make but true *tapisseries* such as the one over our beds. *That* was a gift of an admirer, Mother A said."

Elaine had met Mother Argente the night before. She was a small white-haired woman with soft, plump cheeks and hands that disguised the steel beneath. Elaine wondered who could admire such a firm soul. That kind of firmness quite frightened her.

She spun around to set the whole room into a blur of brown wood and blue coverlets and the bright spots of tapestry wool hanging on the wall. She spun until she was dizzy and had to stop or collapse. The braid fell from her mouth and she stood hands at her side, silently staring.

"Do you have a name yet?" the mist-haired girl asked.

After a moment came the throaty reply. "Elaine."

"No, no, your bird name, she means." The other standing girl, plump and whey-faced, spoke in a twittering voice.

Mist-hair added, "We all receive bird names, new names, like novices in nunneries, until we decide whether to stay. That's because the Druids have their trees and tree alphabet for *their* magic, but we have our little birds who make their living off the trees. That's what Mother A says. It's all in the *Book*. After that, if we stay, we get to have Mother names and live on Holy Isle forever."

"Forever," whispered Elaine. She could not imagine it.

"Do you want to know *our* bird names?" asked whey-face.

Before Elaine could answer, the tall girl said, "I'm Gale— for nightingale—because I sing so well. And this is Marta for house martin because she is our homebody, coming from Shapwick, across the flood. And over there—that . . ." she hesitated a moment, as much to draw a breath as to make a point, "that is Veree. That's because she's solitary like the vireo, and a rare visitor to our isle. At least she's rare in her own eyes." She paused. "We used to have Brambling, but she got sick from the dampness and had to go home or die."

"I didn't like Bram," Marta said. "She was too common and she whined all the time. Mother Hesta couldn't bear her, and that's why she had to leave."

"It was her chest and the bloody cough."

"It was her whine."

"Was not."

"Was."

"Was not."

"Was!"

Veree stood and came over to Elaine who had put the braid back into her mouth during the girls' argument. "Don't let their squabblings fright you," she said gently. "They are chickens scratching over bits of feed. Rumor and gossip excite them."

The braid dropped from Elaine's mouth.

"You think because you're castle born that you're better than we are," scolded Marta. "But all are the same on this holy isle."

Veree smiled. It was not an answer but a confirmation.

"We will see," hissed Gale. "There is still the forging."

"But she's *good* at forging," Marta murmured.

Gale pursed her mouth. "We will see."

Veree ignored them, putting a hand under Elaine's chin and lifting her face until they were staring at one another, gray eyes into violet ones. Elaine could not look away.

"You are quite, quite beautiful," Veree pronounced at last, "and you take in everything with those big eyes. But like the magpie, you give nothing away. I expect they'll call you Maggie, but *I* shall call you Pie."

Beyond the fingers of light cast by the hearth fire was a darkness so thick it seemed palpable. On the edges of the darkness, as it crowded them together, sat the nine Mothers of Ynis Evelonia. In the middle of the half circle, in a chair with a firm back, sat Mother Argente, smiling toward the flames, her fingers busy with needlework. She did not once look down to check the accuracy of her stitches but trusted her fingers to do their work.

"Young Maggie seems to be settling in quite nicely. No crying at night, no outlandish longings for home, no sighing or sniffles. We needn't have been so worried," Her comment did not name any specific worrier, but the Mothers who had voiced such fears to her in the privacy of their morning confessionals were chastized all the same.

Still chaffing over the rejection of her suggested name, Hesta sniffed. "She's too much like Veree—high-strung, coddled. And she fair worships the ground Veree treads which, of course, Veree encourages."

"Now, now, Hesta," Mother Sonda soothed. She made the same sounds to chickens agitated at laying time and buyers in the guest house, a response in tone rather than actual argument. It always worked. Hesta smoothed her skirts much like a preening bird and settled down.

Sonda rose to stack another log onto the embers and to relight a taper on the candlestand. A moth fluttered toward the flame and on reaching it, burst with a sudden bright light. Sonda swept the ashes onto the floor where they disappeared into shadows and rushes. Then, turning, she spoke with a voice as sweetly welcoming as the scent of roses and verbena in the room.

"Mother A has asked me to read the lesson for this evening." She stepped to the lectern where the great leather-bound *Book of Brightness* lay open. Above it, from the sconce on the wall, another larger taper beamed down to light the page. Sonda ran her finger along the text, careful not to touch either the words or the brightly colored illuminations. Halfway, she stopped, looked up, and judging the stilled expectant audience, glanced down again and began to read.

The lesson was short: a paragraph and a parable about constancy. The longer reading had been done before the full company of women and girls at dinner. Those who could took turns with the readings. All others listened. Young Maggie, with her low, steady voice and ability to read phrases rather than merely piece together words, would some day make a fine reader. She would probably make a fine Mother, too. Time—and trial—would tell. That was the true magic on the isle: time and trial.

Sonda looked up from the text for a moment. Mother Argente always chose the evening's lesson. The mealtime reading was done from the *Book*'s beginning straight through to the end. In that way the entire *Book of Brightness* was heard at least once a year by everyone on the isle.

As usual, Sonda was in full agreement with Mother A's choice of the parable on constancy. In the last few months the small community had been beset by inconstancy, as if there were a curse at work, a worm at the heart inching its way to the surface of the body. Four of the novices had left on one pretext or another, a large number in such a short time. One girl with the bloody flux whose parents had desired that she die at home. One girl beset by such lingering homesickness as to render her unteachable. One girl plainly too stupid to learn at all. And one girl summoned home to be married. Married! Merely a piece in her father's game, the game of royalty. Sonda had escaped that game on her own by fasting until her desperate father had given her permission to join the Daughters of Eve. But then, he had had seven other daughters to counter with. And if such losses of novices were not enough— girls were always coming and going—two of the fully vowed women had left as well, one to care for her aged and dying parents and take over the reins of landholding until her brothers might return from war. And one, who had been on the isle for twenty years, had run off with a Cornish miller, a widower only recently bereaved; run off to become his fourth wife. Constancy indeed!

Sonda stood for a moment after the reading was over, her hands lingering on the edges of the *Book*. She loved the feel of it under her fingers, as if the text could impress itself on her by the feel of the parchment alone. She envied mothers Morgan and Marie who could write and illumine the pages. They were at work on a new copy of the *Book* to be set permanently in the dining common so that this one, old and fragile and precious, would not have to be shifted daily.

Finally Sonda took her place again on a stool by Mother A's right hand.

Mother A shifted a moment and patted Sonda's knee. Then she looked to the right and left, taking in all eight women with her glance. "My sisters," she began, "tomorrow our beloved daughter Vireo will begin her steel."

Elaine awoke because someone was crying. She had been so near crying herself for a fortnight that the sound of the quiet weeping set her off, and before she could stop herself, she was snuffling and gulping, the kind of sobbing that Nanny Bess always called "bear grabbers."

She was making so much noise, she did not hear the other weeper stop and move onto her bed, but she felt the sudden warmth of the girl's body and the sturdy arms encircling her.

"Hush, hush, little Pie," came a voice, and immediately after her hair was smoothed down.

Elaine looked up through tear-blurred eyes. There was no moon to be seen through the windows, no candles lit. The dark figure beside her was faceless, but she knew the voice.

"Oh, Veree," she whispered, "I didn't *mean* to cry."

"Nor I, little one. You have been brave the long weeks here. I have seen that and admired it. And now, I fear that I have been the cause of your weeping."

"No, not you, Veree. Never you. It is just that I miss my father so much. And my brother Lavaine, who is the handsomest man in all the world."

Veree laughed and tousled the girl's hair. "Ah, there can be no *handsomest* man, Pie. All men be the same to the women who love and serve the bright goddess flame here."

"If I cannot still love my Lavaine, then I do not want to *be* here." She wiped at her eyes.

"You will get over such losses. I have." Veree sat back on the bed.

"Then why *were* you crying? It was that which woke me." Elaine would admit that much.

Veree shushed her fiercely and glanced around, but the other two girls slept on.

Elaine whispered, "You *were* weeping. By the window. Admit it."

"Yes, sweet Pie, I was crying. But not for the loss of

father or brother. Nor yet for house and land. I cry about tomorrow and tomorrow's morrow, and especially the third day after when I must finish my steel." She rose and went towards the window.

Elaine saw the shadow of her passing betwixt dark and dark and shivered slightly. Then she got out of her bed and the shock of the cold stone beneath the rushes caused her to take quick, short steps over to Veree who sat by the open window.

Outside a strange moaning, part wind and part water, sighed from the Tamor. A night owl on the hunt cried, a soft ascending wheeze of sound.

Elaine put her hand out and touched Veree's shoulder, sturdy under the homespun shift. "But what are you afraid of? Do you fear being burned? Do you fear the blade? I had a maidservant once who turned white as hoarfrost when she had to look upon a knife, silly thing."

"I fear the hurting. I fear . . . the blood."

"What blood?"

In the dark Veree turned and Elaine could suddenly see two tiny points of light flashing out from the shadow eyes. "They have not told you yet about the blood?"

Elaine shook her head. Then realizing the motion might not be read in the blackness, she whispered, "No. Not yet."

Veree sighed, a sound so unlike her that Elaine swallowed with difficulty.

"Tell me. Please."

"I must not."

"But *they* will soon."

"Then let *them*."

"But I must know now so that I might comfort you, who have comforted me these weeks." Elaine took her hand away from Veree's shoulder and reached for a lock of her own hair, unbound from its night plait, and popped it into her mouth, a gesture she had all but forgotten the last days.

"Oh, little Pie, you must not think I am a coward, but if I tell you when I should not . . . I would not have you think me false." Veree's voice was seeped in sadness.

"I never . . ."

"You will when I tell you."

"You are wonderful," Elaine said, proclaiming fealty. "You have been the one to take me in, to talk to me, to listen. The others are all common mouths chattering, empty heads like wooden whistles blowing common tunes." That was one of Nanny Bess' favorite sayings. "Nothing would make me think you false. Not now, not ever."

Veree's head turned back to the window again and the twin points of light were eclipsed. She spoke toward the river and the wind carried her soft words away. Elaine had to strain to hear them.

"Our steel is forged of three of the four elements—fire and water and air."

"I know that."

"But the fourth thing that makes Evian steel, what makes it strike true, is a secret learned by Mother Morgan from a necromancer in the East where magic rides the winds and every breath is full of spirits."

"And what is the fourth thing?" whispered Elaine, though she feared she already knew.

Veree hesitated, then spoke. "Blood. The blood of a virgin girl, an unblemished child, or a childless old maid. Blood drawn from her arm where the vein runs into the heart. The left arm. Here." And the shadow held out its shadowy arm, thrusting it half out of the window.

Elaine shivered with more than the cold.

"And when the steel has been worked and pounded and beaten and shaped and heated, again and again, it is thrust into a silver vat that contains pure water from our well mixed through with the blood."

"Oh." Elaine sighed.

"And the words from the *Book of Brightness* are spoken over it by the mothers in the circle of nine. The sword is pulled from its bloody bath. Then the girl, holding up the sword, with the water flooding down her arm, marches into the Tamor, into the tidal pool that sits in the shadow of the high tor. She must go under the water with the sword, counting to nine times nine. Then thrusting the sword up and out of the water before her, she follows it into the light. Only then is the forging done."

"Perhaps taking the blood will not hurt, Veree. Or only

a little. The mothers are gentle. I burned myself the third day here, and Mother Sonda soothed it with a honey balm and not a scar to show for it."

Veree turned back to the window. "It must be done by the girl all alone at the rising of the moon. Out in the glade. Into the silver cup. And how can I, little Pie, how can I prick my own arm with a knife, I who cannot bear to see myself bleed. Not since I was a small child, could I bear it without fainting. Oh, I can kill spiders, and stomp on serpents. I am not afraid of binding up another's wounds. But my own blood . . . if I had known . . . if my father had known . . . I never would have come."

Into the silence that followed her anguished speech, came the ascending cry of another owl, which ended in a shriek as the bird found its prey. The cry seemed to agitate the two sleepers in their beds and they stirred noisily. Veree and Elaine stood frozen for the moment, and even after were tentative with their voices.

"Could you . . ." Elaine began.

"Yes?"

"Could you use an animal's blood instead?"

"Then the magic would not work and everyone would know."

Elaine let out a long breath. "Then I shall go out in your place. We shall use *my* blood and you will not have to watch." She spoke quite assuredly, though her heart beat wildly at her own suggestion.

Veree hugged her fiercely. "What *can* you think of me that you would believe I would let you offer yourself in my place, little one. But I shall love you forever just for making the suggestion."

Elaine did not quite understand why she should feel so relieved, but she smiled into the darkness. Then she yawned loudly.

"What *am* I thinking of?" Veree chastised herself. "You should be sleeping, little one, not staying up with me. But be relieved. You have comforted me. I think . . ." she hesitated for a little, then finished gaily, "I think I shall manage it all quite nicely now."

"Really?" asked Elaine.

"Really," said Veree. "Trust me."

"I do. Oh, I do," said Elaine and let herself be led back to bed where she fell asleep at once and dreamed of an angel with long dark braids in a white shift who sang, "verily, verily," to her and drew a blood-red crux on her forehead and breast and placed her, ever smiling, in a beautiful silk-lined barge.

If there was further weeping that night, Elaine did not wake to it, nor did she speak of it in the morn.

The morn was the first day of Veree's steel and the little isle buzzed with the news. The nine Mothers left the usual chores to the lesser women and the girls, marching in a solemn line to the forge where they made a great circle around the fire.

In due time Veree, dressed in a white robe with the hood obscuring her face, was escorted by two guides, Mothers who had been chosen by lot. They walked along the Path of Steel, the winding walkway to the smithy that was lined with water-smoothed stones.

As she walked, Veree was unaware of the cacophony of birds that greeted her from the budding apple boughs. She never noticed a flock of finches that rose up before her in a cloud of yellow wings. Instead her head was full of the chant of the sword.

> *Water to cool it,*
> *Forge to heat it,*
> *Anvil to form it,*
> *Hammer to beat it.*

She thought carefully of the points of the sword: hilt and blade, forte and foible, pommel and edge, quillon and grip. She rehearsed her actions. She thought of everything but the blood.

Then the door in front of her opened, and she disappeared inside. The girls who had watched like little birds behind the trees sighed as one.

"It will be your turn next full moon," whispered Marta to Gale. Gale smiled crookedly. The five girls from the other sleeping room added their silent opinions with fingers working small fantasies into the air. Long after the other girls slipped back to their housely duties, Elaine remained, rooted in place. She watched the forge and could only guess at the smoky signals that emerged from the chimney on the roof.

> *Water to cool it,*
> *Forge to heat it,*
> *Anvil to form it,*
> *Hammer to beat it.*

The mothers chanted in perfect unity, their hands clasped precisely over the aprons of their robes. When the chant was done, Mother Argente stepped forward and gently pushed Veree's hood back.

Released from its binding, Veree's hair sprang forward like tiny black arrows from many bowstrings, the dark points haloing her face.

She really is a magnificent child, Argente thought to herself, but aloud spoke coldly. "My daughter," she said, "the metal thanks us for its beating by becoming stronger. So by our own tempering we become women of steel. Will you become one of us?"

"Mother," came Veree's soft answer, "I will."

"Then you must forge well. You must pour your sweat and your blood into this sword that all who see it and any who use it shall know it is of excellent caliber, that it is of Evian Steel."

"Mother, I will."

The Mothers stood back then and only Hesta came forward. She helped Veree remove her robe and the girl stood stiffly in her new forging suit of tunic and trews. Hesta bound her hair back into a single braid, tying it with a golden twine so tightly that it brought tears to the girl's eyes. She blinked them back, making no sound.

"Name your tools," commanded Hesta.

Veree began. Pointing out each where it hung on its hook on the wall, she droned: "Top swage, bottom swage, flatter, cross peen, top fuller, bottom fuller, hot chisel, mandrel..." The catalogue went on and only half her mind was occupied with the rota. This first day of the steel was child's play, things she had memorized her first weeks on Ynis Evelonia and never forgot. They were testing the knowledge of her head. The second day they would test her hands. But the third day . . . she hesitated a moment, looked up, saw that Hesta's eyes on her were glittering. For the first time she understood that the old forge mistress was hoping that she would falter, fail. That startled her. It had never occurred to her that someone she had so little considered could wish her ill.

She smiled a false smile at Hesta, took up the list, and finished it flawlessly.

The circle of nine nodded.

"Sing us now the color of the steel," said Sonda.

Veree took a breath and began. "When the steel is red as blood, the surface is at all points good; and when the steel is rosy red, the top will scale, the sword is dead; and when the steel is golden bright, the time for forging is just right; and when the steel is white as snow, the time for welding you will know."

The plainsong accompaniment had helped many young girls remember the colors, but Veree sang it only to please the mothers and pass their test. She had no trouble remembering when to forge and when to weld, and the rest was just for show.

"The first day went splendidly," remarked Sonda at the table.

"No one ever questioned *that* one's head knowledge," groused Hesta, using her own head as a pointer toward the table where the girls sat.

Mother Argente clicked her tongue against the roof of her mouth, a sound she made when annoyed. The others responded to it immediately with silence, except for Mother Morgan who was so deep in conversation with a server she did not hear.

"We will discuss this later. At the hearth," Argente said.

The conversation turned at once to safer topics: the price of corn, how to raise the milling fee, the prospect of another visitor from the East, the buyer of Veree's sword.

Morgan looked over. "It shall be the arch-mage," she said. "He will come for the sword himself."

Hesta shook her head. "How do you know? How do you *always* know?"

Morgan smiled, the corners of her thin upper lip curling. There was a gap between her two front teeth, carnal, inviting. "I know."

Sonda reached out and stroked the back of Hesta's hand. "You know she would have you think it's magic. But it is the calendar, Hesta. I have explained all that."

Hesta mumbled, pushing the lentils around in her bowl. Her own calendar was internal and had to do with forging, when the steel was ready for the next step. But if Morgan went by any calendar, it was too deep and devious for the forge mistress' understanding. Or for any of them. Morgan always seemed to *know* things. Under the table, Hesta crossed her fingers, holding them against her belly as protection.

"It *shall* be the arch-mage," Morgan said, still smiling her gapped smile. "The stars have said it. The moon has said it. The winds have said it."

"And now you have said it, too." Argente's voice ended the conversation, though she wondered how many of her women were sitting with their fingers crossed surreptitiously under the table. She did not encourage them in their superstitions, but the ones who came from the outer tribes or the lower classes never really rid themselves of such beliefs. "Of course, it shall be a Druid. Someone comes once a year at this time to look over our handiwork. They rarely buy. Druids are as close with their gold as a dragon on its hoard."

"It shall be the arch-mage himself," intoned Morgan. "I know."

Hesta shivered.

"Yes," Argente smiled, almost sighing. When Morgan became stubborn it was always safest to cozen her. Her pharmacopeia was not to be trusted entirely. "But gloating over such arcane knowledge does not become you, a daughter of a queen. I am sure you have more important matters to attend to. Come mothers, I have decided that tonight's reading shall be about humility. And you, Mother Morgan, will do us all the honor of reading it." Irony, Argente had found, was her only weapon against Morgan, who seemed entirely oblivious to it. Feeling relieved of her anger by such petty means always made Argente full of nervous energy. She stood. The others stood with her and followed her out the door.

Elaine watched as Veree marched up to the smithy, this time with an escort of four guides. Veree was without the white robe, her forge suit unmarked by fire or smoke, her hair bound back with the golden string but not as tightly as when Hesta plaited it. Elaine had done the service for her soon after rising, gently braiding the hair and twine together so that they held but did not pull. Veree had rewarded her with a kiss on the brow.

"This day I dedicate to thee," Veree had whispered to her in the courtly language they had both grown up with.

Elaine could still feel the glow of that kiss on her brow. She knew that she would love Veree forever, the sister of her heart. She was glad now, as she had never been before, that she had had only brothers and no sisters in Escalot. That way Veree could be the only one.

The carved wooden door of the smithy closed behind Veree. The girls, giggling, went back to their chores. Only Elaine stayed, straining to hear something of the rites that would begin the second day of Veree's Steel.

Veree knew the way of the steel, bending the heated strips, hammering them together, recutting and rebending them repeatedly until the metal patterned. She knew the sound of the hammer on the hot blade, the smell of the glowing charcoal that made the soft metal hard. She enjoyed the hiss of the quenching, when the hot steel plunged into the water and emerged, somehow, harder still. The day's work was always difficult but satisfying in a way that other work was not. Her hands now held a knowledge that she had not had two years before when, as a pampered young daughter of a baron, she had come to Ynis Evelonia to learn "to be a man as well as a woman" as her father had said. He believed that a woman who might some day have to rule a kingdom (oh, he had such high hopes for her), needed to know both principles, male and female. A rare man, her

father. She did not love him. He was too cold and distant
and cerebral for that. But she admired him. She wanted him
to admire her. And—except for the blood—she was not
unhappy that she had come.

Except for the blood. If she thought about it, her hand
faltered, the hammer slipped, the sparks flew about carelessly and Hesta boomed out in her forge-tending voice
about the recklessness of girls. So Veree very carefully did
not think about the blood. Instead she concentrated on fire
and water, on earth and air. Her hands gripped her work.
She *became* the steel.

She did not stop until Hesta's hand on her shoulder cau-
tioned her.

"It be done for the day, my daughter," Hesta said, grudg-
ing admiration in her voice. "Now you rest. Tonight you
must do the last of it alone."

And then the fear really hit her. Veree began to tremble.

Hesta misread the shivering. "You be aweary with work.
You be hungry. Take some watered wine for sleep's sake.
We mothers will wake you and lead you to the glade at
moonrise. Come. The sword be well worked. You have
reason to be proud."

Veree's stomach began to ache, a terrible dull pain. She
was certain that, for the first time in her life, she would fail
and that her father would be hurt and the others would pity
her. She expected she could stand the fear, and she would,
as always, bear the dislike of her companions, but what
could not be borne was their pity. When her mother had
died in the bloody aftermath of an unnecessary birth, the
entire court had wept and everyone had pitied her, poor little
motherless six-year-old Gwyneth. But she had rejected their
pity, turning it to white anger against her mother who had
gone without a word. She had not accepted pity from any
of those peasants then; she would not accept it now. Not
even from little Pie, who fair worshiped her. Especially not
from Pie.

The moon's cold fingers stroked Veree's face but she did
not wake. Elaine, in her silent vigil, watched from her bed.
She strained to listen as well.

The wind in the orchard rustled the blossoms with a soft

soughing. Twice an owl had given its ascending hunting cry. The little popping hisses of breath from the sleeping girls punctuated the quiet in the room. And Elaine thought that she could also hear, as a dark counter to the other noises, the slapping of the Tamor against the shore, but perhaps it was only the beating of her own heart. She was not sure.

Then she heard the footsteps coming down the hall, hauled the light covers up to her chin, and slotted her eyes.

The Nine Mothers entered the room, their white robes lending a ghostly air to the proceedings. They wore the hoods up, which obscured their faces. The robes were belted with knotted golden twine; nine knots on each cincture and the golden ornament shaped like a circle with one half filled in, the signet of Ynis Evelonia, hanging from the end.

The Nine surrounded Veree's bed, undid their cinctures, and lay the ropes over the girl's body as if binding her to a bier.

Mother Argente's voice floated into the room. "We bind thee to the isle. We bind thee to the steel. We bind thee to thy task. Blood calls to blood, like to like. Give us thine own for the work."

The Nine picked up their belts and tied up their robes once again. Veree, who had awakened some time during Argente's chant, was helped to her feet. The Mothers took off her shift and slipped a silken gown over her head. It was sleeveless and Elaine, watching, shivered for her.

Then Mother Morgan handed her a silver cup, a little grail with the sign of the halved circle on the side. Mother Sonda handed her a silken bandage. Marie bound an illumined message to her brow with a golden headband. Mothers Bronwyn and Matilde washed her feet with lilac water, while Katwyn and Lisanor tied her hair atop her head into a plaited crown. Mother Hesta handed her a silver knife, its tip already consecrated with wine from the Goddess Arbor.

Then Argente put her hands on Veree's shoulders. "May She guide your hand. May She guard your blood. May the moon rise and fall on this night of your consecration. Be you steel tonight."

They led her to the door and pushed her out before them. She did not stumble as she left.

* * *

Veree walked into the glade as if in a trance. She had drunk none of the wine but had spilled it below her bed knowing that the wine was drugged with one of Mother Morgan's potions. Bram had warned her of it before leaving. Silly, whiny Bram who, nonetheless, had had an instinct for gossip and a passion for Veree. Such knowledge had been useful.

The moon peeped in and out of the trees, casting shadows on the path, but Veree did not fear the dark. This night the dark was her friend.

She heard a noise and turned to face it, thinking it some small night creature on the prowl. There was nothing larger than a stoat or fox on Ynis Evelonia. She feared neither. At home she had kept a reynard, raised up from a kit, and had hunted with two ferrets as companions in her pocket.

Home! What images suddenly rose up to plague her, the same that had caused her no end of sleepless nights when she had first arrived. For she *had* been homesick, whatever nonsense she had told little Pie for comfort's sake. The great hearth at Carmelide, large enough to roast an oxen, where once she had lost the golden ring her mother had given her and her cousin Cadoc had grabbed up a bucket of water, dousing the fire and getting himself all black with coal and grease to recover it for her. And the great apple tree outside her bedroom window up which young Jemmy, the ostler's son, had climbed to sing of his love for her even though he knew he would be soundly beaten for it. And the mews behind the main house where Master Thom had kept the hawks and let her sneak in to practice holding the little merlin that she had wanted for her own. But it had died tangled in its jesses the day before she'd been sent off to the isle, and one part of her had been glad that no one else would hunt the merlin now.

She heard the noise again, louder this time, too loud for a fox or a squirrel or a stoat. Loud enough for a human. She spoke out, "Who is it?" and held out the knife before her, trembling with the cold. Only the cold, she promised herself.

"It is I," came a small voice.

"Pie!" Her own voice took back its authority. "You are not supposed to be here."

"I saw it all, Veree. The dressing and undressing. The ropes and the knife. And I *did* promise to help." The childish form slipped out from behind the tree, white linen shift reflecting the moon's light.

"I told you all would be well, child. You did not need to come."

"But I *promised*." If that voice held pity, it was self-pity. The child was clearly a worshiper begging not to be dismissed.

Veree smiled and held out the hand with the cup. "Come, then. Thou shalt be my page."

Elaine put her hand to Veree's gown and held on as if she would never let go and, so bound, the two entered into the Goddess Glade.

The arch-mage came in the morning just as Morgan had foretold. He was not at all what Elaine had expected, being short and balding, with a beard as long and as thin as an exclamation mark. But that he was a man of power no one could doubt.

The little coracle, rowed by the same ferret-faced woman who had deposited Elaine on the isle, fair skimmed the surface of the waves and plowed onto the shore, leaving a furrow in which an oak could have been comfortably set.

The arch-mage stood up in the boat and greeted Mother Argente familiarly. *"Salve, mater. Visne somnia vendere?"*

She answered him back with great dignity. *"Si volvo, Merline, caveat emptor."*

Then they both laughed, as if this exchange were a great and long-standing joke between them. If it was a joke, they were certainly the only ones to understand it.

"Come, Arch-Mage," Mother Argente said, "and take wine with us in the guest house. We will talk of the purpose of your visit in comfort there."

He nodded and, with a quick twist of his wrist, produced a coin from behind the boat woman's right ear. With a flourish he presented it to her, then stepped from the coracle. The woman dropped the coin solemnly into the leather bag she wore at her waist.

Elaine gasped and three other girls giggled.

"The girls are, as always, amused by your tricks, Merlin," said Mother Argente, her mouth pursed in a wry smile.

"I like to keep in practice," he said. "*And* to amuse the young ones. Besides, as one gets older the joints stiffen."

"That I know, that I know," Argente agreed. They walked side by side like old friends, moving slowly up the little hill. The rest of the women and girls fell in behind them, and so it was, in a modest processional, that they came to the guest house.

At the door of the wattle pavilion which was shaded by a lean of willows, Mother Argente turned. "Sonda, Hesta, Morgan, Lisanor, enter and treat with our guest. Veree, ready yourself for noon. The rest of you, you know your duties." Then she opened the door and let Merlin precede them into the house.

The long table was already set with platters of cheese and fruit. Delicate goblets of Roman glass marked off six places. As soon as they were all seated with Argente at the head and Merlin at the table's foot, Mother A poured her own wine and passed the silver ewer. Morgan, seated at Argente's right hand, was the last to fill her glass. When she set the ewer down, she raised her glass.

"I am Wind on Sea," Morgan chanted.

> "I am Wind on Sea,
> I am Ocean-wave,
> I am Roar of Sea,
> I am Bull of Seven Fights,
> I am Vulture on Cliff,
> I am Dewdrop,
> I am Fairest of Flowers,
> I am Boar for Boldness,
> I am Salmon in Pool,
> I am Lake on Plain,
> I am a Word of Skill
> I am the Point of a Weapon—"

"Morgan" warned Argente.

"Do not stop her," commanded Merlin. "She is *vates*, afire with the word of the Gods. My god or your god, they are the same. They speak with tongues of fire and they sometimes pick a warped reed through which to blow a particular tune."

Argente bowed her head once to him but Morgan was already finished. She looked across the table at Hesta, her eyes preternaturally bright. "I know things." she said.

"It is clear that I have come at a moment of great power," said Merlin. "'I am the point of a Weapon' say the gods to us. And my dreams these past months have been of sword point, but swords that are neither *gladius* nor *spatha* nor the far tribes' *ensis*. A new creation. And where does one come for a sword of power, but here. Here to Ynis Evelonia."

Mother Argente smiled. "We have many swords ready, arch-mage."

"I need but one." He did not return her smile, staring instead into his cup of wine.

"How will we know this sword of power?" Argente asked, leaning forward.

"I will know," intoned Morgan.

Sonda, taking a sip of her wine, put her head to one side like a little bird considering a tasty worm. "And what payment, arch-mage?"

"Ah, Mother Sonda, that is always the question they leave to you. What payment indeed." Merlin picked up his own glass and suddenly drained it. He set the glass down gently, contemplating the rim. Then he stroked his long beard. "If I dream true—and I have never been known to have false dreams—then you shall *give* me this particular sword and its maker."

"*Give* you? What a notion, Merlin." Mother Argente laughed, but there was little amusement in it. "The swords made of Evian Steel are never given away. We have too many buyers vying for them. If you will not pay for it, there will be others who will."

There was a sudden, timid knock upon the door. Sonda rose quietly and went to it, spoke to the Mother who had interrupted them, then turned.

"It is nearing noon, Mother. The sun rides high. It is time." Sonda's voice was smooth, giving away no more than necessary.

Mother Argente rose and with her the others rose, too.

"Stay, Arch-Mage, there is food and wine enough. When we have done with our . . . obsequies . . . we shall return to finish our business with you."

The five Mothers left and so did not hear the man murmur into his empty cup, "This business will be finished before-times."

The entire company of women gathered at the river's edge to watch. The silver vat, really an overlarge bowl, was held by Mother Morgan. The blood-tinted water reflected only sky.

Veree, in the white silken shift, stood with her toes curling under into the mud. Elaine could see the raised goose bumps along her arms, though it was really quite warm in the spring sun.

Mother Hesta held a sword on the palms of her upturned hands. It was a long-bladed double edge sword, the quillon cleverly worked. The sword seemed afire with the sun, the shallow hollow down its center aflame.

Veree took the sword from Hesta and held it flat against her breast while Mother Argente anointed her forehead with the basin's water. With her finger she drew three circles and three crosses on Veree's brow.

"Blood to blood, steel to steel, thee to me," said Mother Argente.

Veree repeated the chant. "Blood to blood, steel to steel, I to thee." Then she took the sword and set it into the basin.

As the sword point and then the blade touched the water, the basin erupted in steam. Great gouts of fire burst from the sword and Mother Argente screamed.

Veree grabbed the sword by the handle and ran down into the tidal pool. She plunged in with it and immediately the flames were quenched, but she stayed under the water and Elaine, fearful for her life, began to cry out, running down to the water's edge.

She was pushed aside roughly by a strong hand and when she caught her breath, she saw it was the arch-mage himself, standing knee deep in water, his hands raised, palms down, speaking words she did not quite understand.

"I take ye here
Till Bedevere
Cast ye back."

Bedevere? Did he mean Veree? Elaine wondered, and
then had time to wonder no further for the waters parted
before the arch-mage and the sword pierced up into the air
before him.

He grasped the pommel in his left hand and with a mighty
heave pulled the sword from the pool. Veree's hand, like
some dumb, blind thing, felt around in the air, searching.

Elaine waded in, dived under, and wrapping her arms
around Veree's waist, pushed her out of the pool. They stood
there, trembling, looking like two drowned ferrets, unable
to speak or weep or wonder.

"This is the sword I shall have," Merlin said to Mother
Argente, his back to the two half-drowned girls.

"I do not understand . . ." began Mother Argente. "But
I *will* know."

"I *know* things," said Morgan triumphantly.

Mother Argente turned and spoke through clenched teeth,
"Will someone shut her up?"

Hesta smiled broadly. "Yes, Mother. Your will is my
deed." Her large right hand clamped down on Morgan's
neck and she picked her up and shook her like a terrier with
a rat, then set her down. Morgan did not speak again but
her eyes grew slotted and cold.

Marta began to sob quietly until nudged by Gale, but the
other girls were stunned into silence.

"Now, now," murmured Sonda to no one in particular.
"Now, now."

Mother Argente walked over to Veree who straightened
up and held her chin high. "Explain this, child."

Veree said nothing.

"What blood was used to quench the sword?"

"Mother, it was my own."

Elaine interrupted. "It was. I saw it."

Mother Argente turned on her. "You *saw* it? Then it was
your watching that corrupted the steel."

Merlin moved between them. "*Mater*. Think. Such power

does not emanate from this child." He swung his head so
that he was staring at Veree. "And where did the blood come
from?"

Under his stare Veree lowered her eyes. She spoke to
the ground. "It is a woman's secret. I cannot talk of it."

The arch-mage smiled. "I am man and woman, neither
and both. The secrets of the body are known to me. Nothing
is hidden from me."

"I have nothing to tell you if you know it already."

"Then I will tell it to thee," said Merlin. He shifted the
sword to his left hand, turned to her, and put his right hand
under her chin. "Look at me, Gwyneth, called here Vireo,
and deny this if you can. Last night for the first time you
became a woman. The moon called out your blood. And it
was this flux that you used, the blood that flows from the
untested womb, not the body's blood flowing to the heart.
Is it so?"

She whispered, "It is so."

Argente put a hand to her breast. "That is foul. Unclean."

"It is the more powerful thereby," Merlin answered.

"Take the sword, arch-mage. And the girl. And go."

"*No!*" Elaine dropped to her knees by Veree's side and
clasped her legs. "Do not go. Or take me with you. I could
not bear to be here without you. I would die for you."

Merlin looked down at the little girl and shook his head.
"You shall not die yet, little Elaine. Not so soon. But you
shall give your life for her—that I promise you." He tucked
the sword in a scabbard he suddenly produced from inside
his cloak. "Come, Gwyneth." He held out his hand.

She took his hand and smiled at him. "There is nothing
here to pity," she said.

"I shall never give you pity," he said. "Not now or ever.
You choose and you are chosen. I see that you know what
it is you do."

Mother Argente smoothed her skirts down, a gesture
which seemed to return them all to some semblance of
normality. "I myself will row you across. The sooner she
is gone from here, the better."

"But my clothes, mother."

"They shall be sent to you."

The arch-mage swung the cape off his shoulders and enfolded the girl in it. The cape touched the ground, sending up little puffs of dirt.

"You shall never be allowed on this isle again," said Mother Argente. "You shall be denied the company of women. Your name shall be crossed off the book of the Goddess."

Veree still smiled.

"You shall be barren," came a voice from behind them. "Your womb's blood was given to cradle a sword. It shall not cradle a child. I *know* things."

"Get into the boat," instructed Merlin. "Do not look back, it only encourages her." He spoke softly to Mother Argente, "I am glad, *Mater* that *that* one is *your* burden."

"I give you no thanks for her," said Mother Argente as she pushed the boat off into the tide. She settled onto the seat, took up the oars, feathered them once, and began to pull.

The coracle slipped quickly across the river.

Veree stared out across the gray waters that gave scarcely any reflection. Through the mist she could just begin to see the far shore where the tops of thatched cottages and the smoky tracings of cook fires were taking shape.

"Shapwick-across-the-flood," mused Merlin. "And from there we shall ride by horse to Camlann. It will be a long and arduous journey, child. Your bones will ache."

"Pitying me already?"

"Pitying *you?* My bones are the older and will ache the more. No, I will not pity you. But we will all be pitied when this story is told years hence, for it will be a tale cunningly wrought of earth, air, fire—and blood."

The boat lodged itself clumsily against the Shapwick shore. The magician stood and climbed over the side. He gathered the girl up and carried her to the sand, huffing mightily. Then he turned and waved to the old woman who huddled in the coracle.

"*Ave, mater.*"

"*Ave, magister,*" she called back, "Until we must meet again."

* * *

Ynis Evelonia, the Isle of Women, lies within the marshy tidal river Tamor that is itself but a ribbon stretched between the Mendip and the Quantock hills. The isle is scarcely remarked from the shore. It is as if Manannan MacLir himself had shaken his cloak between.

On most days there is an unsettling mist obscuring the irregular coast of the isle; and only in the full sun, when the light just rising illuminates a channel, can any passage across the glass-colored waters be seen. And so it is that women alone, who have been schooled in the hidden causeways across the fen, mother to daughter down through the years, can traverse the river in coracles that slip easily through the brackish flood.

By ones and twos they come and go in their light skin boats to commerce with the Daughters of Eve who stay in holy sistership on the isle, living out their chaste lives and making with their magics the finest blades mankind has ever known.

The isle is dotted with trees, not the great Druidic oaks that line the roadways into Godney and Meare and tower over the mazed pathways up to the high tor, but small womanish trees: alder and apple, willow and ash, leafy havens for the migratory birds. And the little isle fair rings with bird song and the clanging of hammer on anvil and steel.

But men who come to buy swords at Ynis Evelonia are never allowed further inland than the wattle guest house with its oratory of wicker wands winded and twisted together under a rush roof. Only one man has ever slept there and is—in fact—sleeping there still. But that is the end of this story—which shall not be told—and the beginning of yet another.

... it fell so that Merlin fell in a dotage on the damosel that King Pellinore brought to court, and she was one of the damosels of the lake, that hight Nimue. But Merlin would let her have no rest, but always he would be with her. And ever she made Merlin good cheer till she learned of him all manner thing that she desired; and he was assotted upon her, that he might not be from her.

—Le Morte D'Arthur
by Sir Thomas Malory

In the
Whitethorn Wood

He woke to wood and the underside of bark. There had been no death, at least none that he remembered. Just a long, final breath, part kiss and part spell. A name formed on his mouth, a name he could not quite shape, though he was sure it began with an *n*.

"Nnnnn," he murmured tentatively.

Reaching upward, his hands touched wood. He felt wood on all sides, a coffin of it, rounded without the square, hammered pegs. Pushing desperately against it, he was surprised that it had a give to it, as of a living thing. He scratched it with his fingernails and a soft, meaty substance peeled downward.

"Where am I?" he cried out, his words strangely muffled.

In the dark. It was a woman's voice that answered him, but not aloud. *In the dark.*

Where is this dark? he thought to himself, hesitating to frame the question with his mouth.

It did not matter. The woman's voice, low and throaty, still answered him. *In the wood.*

In the dark. In the wood. Bottled up like a cask of wine. They were answers that meant nothing to him. But remembering little else, he knew he was a man used to riddles. They had been—of this one thing he was sure—his life-work. He had moved from riddle to answer, from answer to riddle down through his days. In this dark and in this wood he would unravel this final riddle. And then, like a weaver woman with a fleece, skirting the bad parts and spinning out the thread, he would wind it up again.

He framed a third question in his mind. *What wood?*

The answer came with a laugh. *Whitethorn, old one. And now you have had your three. A magic number for a magic maker.* The laugh died away as quietly as a breeze quits the tops of trees.

Woods. Whitethorn. Dark. But she had given away more than that. He raised his hands once again, bringing them to his useless eyes. Dark only met dark.

Old one, she had said. Was he old? He did not feel old, but then he was not sure he felt anything at all. He touched himself, having no memory of age or time's noisy passage in this silent place. There was only the dark and this *now*. His hands traveled down his face, feeling a beard that fell, a waterfall of hair, twixt nipples and waist. It must have taken a lifetime to grow such a beard.

A tale came to him suddenly: Dead men's hair grows long in the casket. And here he was casked up, old dead wine in a tun. But she had not called him dead—merely old. How long, then, must a man live for such hair to measure him? He could not guess how long.

His hands traveled back up to his face, two friends on a familiar journey. They traced the lines around his mouth, around his eyes. The mouth lines bespoke tragedies, the eye lines laughter. Which were the greater? In the dark it was impossible to tell.

He guided the faithful hands on their journey over his clothes. The jerkin was simply made, but the stitches were tiny and carefully done. The cloth of his shirt was fine. Was he such a master tailor, then, that he could sew such a seam? Or had he had servants at his command?

The hands, like withered leaves in the fall, fell away. Sorrow overrode him. He could not remember. All that was left to him was a kiss and a spell, and a name that began with a murmur. He wept.

He woke again and had no more than the list of wood, dark, whitethorn, old. But then he thought: There was something more she had said. And then he had it, as if a taper had suddenly been lit in the dark. He closed his eyes against the sudden illumination.

Magic. No—*magic maker*. That was what she called him. He snapped his fingers then to see if he could spark magic from them. The only light was the mind's taper and the name she had given him so unwittingly. *Magic maker*.

He thought to himself: What is a magic maker but a mage? A mage deals in images, the prestidigitation of the mind: imagination. Mage, magic, image, imagination. It was all the same. Well, then, if he was a magic maker—and an old one at that—surely he had buried inside him, deeper even than the amnesia in which her dark sorceries had buried him, some small bright images of his past. He would force them up, like buds the gardeners brought to blossom in early spring, past the strictures of her ensorcelment, past the fierce bindings of the whitethorn wood.

The unlucky whitethorn, the maytree, it came to him now. It was the tree of forced chastity and what could be chaster than he, dryadlike, bound up in a tree. His hands went to his face again and he wept.

No! The despair he felt was too black to be real, for it was blacker than even the dark of his wood tomb. It was more enchantment, then, and knowing this, he fought it; he fought with the only magic he still had, the buried images of his past.

Like a fisher lad with a new line, he hooked a berry to the thread and dropped it into the stream of memory. First it floated, bobbing in the current, then suddenly disappeared. He hauled on it and pulled up a picture.

It was of a child, still red with birth blood, lying in his arms. A child with a star that burned on his forehead for a moment, then faded into a birthmark like a faceted jewel.

Was I this child? he asked himself. But the image was too sharp to be a construct. He would not have known himself as a babe. It was a child, then, that he had carried.

Yet he knew himself to be neither mother nor father. Neither, yet both. More riddles.

He looked again at the picture of the babe he had carried, but the picture had dried up around the edges; unsapped, it vanished slowly like dew drawn up from the grass.

A babe. The dark. In the whitethorn wood. Old magic maker. And a name that murmured like a spell. He fought sleep but it overpowered him, and in the sleep there came a dream.

A bear walked by a cleft rock. From behind that rock slipped an asp. The asp wound itself around the bear's legs, touched its genitals, slipped over its back, circled its head like a crown. The bear rose on its hind legs and slapped at the viper. It broke the serpent's back but the poisoned fangs buried in the bear's paw. Bear and asp fell backward into the rock's cleft and disappeared. The rock clanged shut with a knell that woke the dreamer.

It was still dark and his eyes, like hollows, filled with tears.

He set out the pieces he had; counters in a riddling game, moving them around in his mind to force the associations: the deathlike dark, the unlucky whitethorn, old magic maker, the star child, the slotted rock, the bear, and snake. Like the tarot, corrupted by charlatans and played by fools, the images danced busily in his head. He could make no more of them. The riddle, it seemed, was too knotted for his unraveling.

What—he asked himself—did the king of Phyrgia do with such a knot? for the story, first told to him by an old centurion made friendly by wine, came unbidden to his mind. Did the king hope to unwind the knot? No, rather he struck it with his sword, severing the strands forever.

Sword! And with that final image, the answer came to

him, as riddle answers always do, in a final bright shout. Sword bridged babe and rock, contained both bear and asp. It was made of earth and air, fire and water; it was human magic far greater than his own small feats of the mind.

He knew now who he was and who had kissed him and what the spell. The bonds of the whitethorn no longer held him. He spoke the name of the mistress of this magic and severed their ties for all time.

"Nimue," he cried out, and shut his eyes against the sudden light.

"Old man, silly old riddler," came the throaty, laughing voice. "You certainly are persistent. It has taken you centuries to find me out and by now you are surely as shriveled and as chaste as any maytree stick. I fear your advances no longer. In the years between, my magic has o'ergrown yours. Silly old man, do you still want a kiss as your reward?"

She laughed again. Then, puzzled by his continued silence, pulled aside her cloak and was visible at once.

On the ground by the ancient whitethorn that was shriven apart as if by lightning, was a pile of fine white bones. As she watched, the bones sorted themselves into the most complicated magical pattern of all: that of a small man, hands crossed over his chest. The bones were touched suddenly by a light as brilliant as that of starshine, and then in a moment light and bones were gone.

Yet some men say in many parts of England that King Arthur is not dead, but had by the will of our Lord Jesu into another place; and men say that he shall come again, and he shall win the holy cross. I will not say it shall be so, but rather I will say: here in this world he changed his life. But many men say that there is written upon his tomb this verse: HIC JACET ARTHURUS, REX QUONDAM, REXQUE FUTURUS.

—Le Morte D'Arthur
by Sir Thomas Malory

Epitaph

Pushing through the muddled lines of protesters was the easy part, but the noise of their chanting was deafening. It was part English, part some other older language.

The three reporters ran up the marble stairs, leaving the crowds of (mostly) young banner wavers behind a solid police line. But the sound of the chants bounced off the stone stairs and the towering pillars of the courthouse.

McNeil of Reuters laughed as he ran. He smoked too much and was two dozen pounds overweight, but women always seemed to find him attractive. The Irish charm, his great intensity when talking about things that mattered to him, and the slight odor of danger he emitted were inescapable. "Haven't heard that much pure animal noise since Zimbabwe in '93," he shouted at his companions when he reached the top of the stairs.

Patti Pritzkau, "Pretty Patti" as she was known by her *Newsweek* colleagues, was waiting for him. She put her hand on his arm. "I especially like the boy carrying the sign Let's Keep the Myth in Mystery," she said.

"Rhodes scholars no doubt," mumbled McNeil, aware of her hand.

Last up was the dark-haired Stevens of the *Latin American Herald*. Though Jewish and a New Yorker, he affected a Latino mustache in the hopes of improving both his Spanish and his standing among Third World correspondents. "I liked Remember That Mage is in the Middle of Imagination. Good sentiment."

"But lousy mathematics," said Pritzkau. "Mage is nowhere near the middle." She looked at McNeil. "I thought you Brits prided yourselves on your classical educations." Leaning against one of the pillars she watched the crowd.

Stevens snapped a few quick pictures.

"Don't blame *me* for British education," Mac said. "Remember—I'm Irish!" He smiled, part imp, part innocent.

Patti held up her hands. "Okay, Mac, just don't shoot that charm at me." They had been flirting for three months but not gotten past the public stage.

"Come on," Stevens urged. "The conference is scheduled for noon and it's a few minutes past that now. We're the last."

"Typical British attention to time," Patti said over her shoulder as she pushed open the heavy wooden doors. "Be punctual—and a hundred years behind the times."

Behind her the two men laughed and then followed her through the doors into the long, cold, high-ceilinged hall. As they walked toward the Hatfield Room, where the press conference was to take place, Mac reached out for Patti's hand. She let him hold it for a moment, then drew it away.

"Now, now, Mac," she whispered. "That's not professional."

"Your profession—or mine?" he asked with a big grin.

Stevens smothered a laugh. He'd been watching the slow progress of their romance since Pritzkau had arrived from the States. In fact the entire foreign press corps had a bet on it. Stevens' money was on Patti. She reminded him of his oldest sister.

"If we don't hurry," Stevens interrupted, "it will be like coming into a movie halfway through. We'll recognize the actors but have to reconstruct the plot."

They started to trot down the hall and Patti, even in a skirt and low heels, took the lead.

And that, Stevens thought to himself, *is why my money is on her. She's a reporter first and a lover second.*

Mac reached the door last. Between puffs, he said to them, "Relax. Don't hurry so. King Arthur will wait. He's waited all these years, and Merlin, too, to return when we need him. That's the way the story goes. And I, for one, believe it."

"The Irish are great believers," said Stevens.

"And great lovers, too," added Mac with a wink. He laughed and opened the door, bowing low, to let both Pritzkau and Stevens precede him.

In fact the conference had only just begun, with some minor dignitaries standing up for recognition: Oppenheim who headed Arts and Monuments, Turner who ran the Oxbridge Archeology Consortium, and Kotker whose domain was the Bodleian Ancient Manuscripts Section. McNeil pointed them out, adding, "Heavy academic canons."

"Oh, lord," Stevens muttered in a fair imitation of the current prime minister's high-pitched esthete's voice. "And I thought this was going to be words of one syllable."

The trio of scholars sat down in the front row, and the Prince of Wales stepped forward to take the microphone. "It is my great pleasure to introduce a man who has made a discovery that has raised England once again to the glory of its past. A man who..."

McNeil's voice overtook the prince's so that the three or four reporters closest to him missed HRH's next few sentences. "I hear Wales underwrote the expedition. Seems he fell under Stewart's spell at Cambridge. Friends of mine there say the man's a genius at converting undergraduates."

"And the prince being a perennial undergraduate..." added Pritzkau.

"He may have a tougher bunch here today," Stevens said.

"Look around you," Patti stage-whispered, "and then repeat that!"

McNeil smothered a laugh.

The prince had just finished his introduction and the other man at the table stood. He was extremely tall and elegant-looking with thick straight white hair almost to his shoulders. *Leonine* was the word that sprang into the minds of a half-dozen reporters simultaneously. His head seemed almost too large for the long thin body, and when he walked to the microphone, it was with the slight stoop that men affect who grow too quickly in adolescence.

"What great cheekbones," Pritzkau said as the two men shook hands.

"Thank you, ladies and gentlemen of the press. And thank you, Your Royal Highness, for that introduction. My fellow scholars, please forgive me if I step on your illustrious toes or borrow some of your words without full credit in the story that follows. In my printed version, things will be liberally sprinkled with the proper citations and footnotes." He smiled broadly and was rewarded with a friendly wave of chuckles.

"You will all have been handed a sheet of paper as you entered with the historical and literary data on King Arthur and the Matter of Britain as we now know it. That should help any of you who are a bit far away from your school or university courses, and a quick trot for those of us who think we have it all down pat in an easily recallable form."

McNeil whispered to Patti, "Nicely put."

"You mean, not bad for an Englishman?" She said it without turning toward him, but she knew it amused him because he snorted.

After waiting a beat, McNeil whispered directly into her ear, "Scots, actually."

Stewart continued smoothly above the sounds of rustling papers. "What I am going to tell you today may astound some of you, baffle others, and make the cynics among you laugh. *At first.* But I think that by the time I have shown you everything, you will believe, as I believe, that Merlin-nus Ambrosius, aka Myrddin the bard of Gwythheyrn, aka Myrddn Wyllt, aka Merlin the arch-mage, was more than an ordinary run-of-the-mill Celtic soothsayer out of the folk tradition but was rather an unusual, perhaps even extra-ordinary man who lived in sixth century England."

There was little reaction to this introduction, for word of the find had already slipped out in bits and pieces over the long, hot, essentially newsless summer. *People* magazine had carried a gossipy piece on Dr. Stewart's love life (estranged wife once his student, no mistresses). The British yellow sheets had had a field day with the prince's special interest in the discovery of the tomb. And there had been a lot of speculation in the American newsweeklies, as well as long think-pieces in the Italian, French and, surprisingly, Yugoslavian papers. An hour's special on American television was planned.

Stevens folded the handout into halves over and over until the paper was no bigger than his thumb. "My sisters would love this," he muttered to McNeil. "They all read science fiction. But what am I doing here? I'm an economics reporter."

"Wait till you see the Merlin the Magician dolls that will come out this year," McNeil told him. "It will make yo-yos, Hula Hoops, Rubik's Cube, and Cabbage Patch dolls seem like nothing. *That's* economics."

The lights went out and a screen was lowered by some unseen but cranky mechanism. A slide map of Great Britain suddenly appeared before them.

Dr. Stewart's voice floated effortlessly above them. "Was there really a Merlin? It is the very first question we have to ask ourselves. Some authorities hold that the story of Merlin began with a blunder: the mistaken interpretation of the place name 'Carmarthen' as *caer* or town of Myrddin. And because this view was so persuasive, for many years the figure of the arch-mage Merlin has been seen as a folk-loric counterpart of Puck and Queen Mab and Robin Good-fellow, merely the result of spurious etymology.

"But I grew up near the site of ancient Carmarthen, and we boys all took turns standing on a great old tree stump and reciting the local rhymed prophecy: *When Merlin's tree shall tumble down, then shall fall Carmarthen town.* Well, tree and old town were gone, we knew not when or how. So if that was true, then in our boys' hearts, all the rest was true, too."

A light rod pointed to the small dot marked Carmarthen on the map.

"I studied Arthurian literature at the university, a choice probably informed by boyhood dreams, but. . . "

"Which university, sir?" someone called out into the dark.

"Oxford," came the reply.

"Score one," McNeil replied.

Pritzkau giggled. She didn't like the fact; it seemed to rebound on her professionalism. But she giggled.

"And the dons, though lovers of literature, were at the same time great debunkers of myth. They were careful to place Merlin in the Scottish or Welsh or Breton woods as purely a product of the uncultivated folk mind.

"I, however, did not. To me it did not matter if much that was credited to Merlin—for example the prophesies for King Vortigern about the red and white dragons, or the mysterious three laughs the magician made at court—were straight out of traditional tales. Such embroideries always attach themselves to any figure of power. Look what has happened to figures closer to us in time: Napoleon, Lincoln, Churchill, Hitler. All have gathered in their wake a folklore fed by both their followers and their victims.

"No, I was not deterred by the folk additions. I was *encouraged* by them. Just as Heinrich Schliemann was convinced of the core truth of the *Odyssey* and found the fabled treasure of Troy that proved it, I was convinced that in the stories of Arthur's court, the figure of Merlin had been real."

A new slide replaced the map, a montage of wizards as drawn by a variety of artists.

"Well, I recognize Burne-Jones, I think," said Pritzkau.

"There's a Frazetta there. A Tom Canty. A Brian Froud. And the Brothers Hildebrandt," whispered Stevens. Into the stunned silence that followed, he added to his two companions, "Well, my sisters collect the stuff. . . ."

From the front of the room, oblivious to the whisperings of reporters trying to identify the artists, Stewart continued. "There was a lot of material to sift through. Stories, poems, ballads, folklore. . . "

"Bull droppings," Stevens muttered in Spanish.

Pritzkau elbowed him in the side.

"And there were many places identified as Merlin's burial

ground. Merlin Wyllt—Merlin the Wild Man—was said to
have been buried at Bardsey, the island of Welsh saints in
North Wales. Another tradition was that he was buried where
he had been born, on the Ile de Sein off the Breton coast.
Geoffrey of Monmouth's idea was that Merlin had been
buried in a cave at Tintagel. Another popular guess was
Drummelzier on the Tweed." A new map marked with all
the sites slid into view.

"And another legend, which we dismissed out of hand,
was that Merlin had been seen by Irish monks sailing west-
ward in a skiff of crystal. That seemed to me more an
advertising campaign for Waterford than a reasonable ex-
planation for Merlin's disappearance."

"We all know how tricky it is to sail a glass boat in the
Atlantic," called out a reporter in front of Stevens.

The entire auditorium broke into laughter, led by Stewart.

Letting the laughter die down naturally, Stewart took a
moment to shuffle his notes. When it was quiet again, he
said, "The two most persistent stories—rumors if you will—
were that Merlin had been ensorceled or bound up in a tree
and that he had been bewitched under a stone. I took that
to mean burial in a wooden, probably oak, casket or inter-
ment in a cave. I had great hopes for the latter. In temperate
climates such as ours the cool dryness of caves has often
accidentally but quite efficiently embalmed the dead. Such
natural mummies have been found in widely divergent
places—Kiev, Vienna, Venzone (there were two dozen natural mummies discovered in vaults beneath the church). In
Palermo, in catacombs under the town, thousands of such
remains have been found."

Pritzkau was scribbling frantically in the dim light, as
was Stevens. But McNeil sat listening intently, a small,
admiring smile on his face.

The slides went by in quick succession now. Dr. Stewart
pronounced the names of towns and cities where natural
mummies had been unearthed, and the grotesque but oddly
unmoving pictures flashed one after another. "Kiev (click),
Vienna (click click), Venzone (click click click), Palermo
(click click click click click), Chile (click), Wyoming
(click)." The last slide remained, a close-up of a mummified
face, grinning toothily.

"We know that Venzone owes its mummies to something more than just the cooling action of the crypts. There is a local fungus in the cave that also serves to dehydrate. And in some of the American caves, where the remains of Indians have been found, the mummification process was helped along by sodium salts and other compounds in the soil."

The lights came on abruptly.

"Are there any questions so far?" Stewart asked, looking carefully over the crowd.

McNeil raised his hand.

"Yes—the gentleman in the fifth row."

Standing, McNeil nodded. "McNeil. Of Reuters," he said. "Is there evidence of mummification being a process common in Britain at the time of Arthur?"

"Thank you, Mr. McNeil. I am glad you asked that. It leads right into my next point."

"Shill!" Pritzkau said loudly, and the reporters chuckled.

"By the time of Arthur, the early Bronze barrows and cairns had given way to stone vaults and wooden caskets. The idea of true mummification, as practiced by the Egyptians, was unknown to the British tribes. In fact, the word *mummy* did not even enter into English writing until nearly the fourteenth century. It comes from the Latin *mummia* meaning 'mummy powder' which itself came from the Egyptian word for 'pitch.' Within two centuries, mummy powder was being used in Britain and the Continent for curing everything from wrinkle lines to TB, and reputed to be an aphrodisiac besides."

"Great if you're into dead bodies!" hissed Stevens.

"Economics," McNeil reminded him.

As if to prove McNeil's point, Dr. Stewart added, "Newly dug-up mummies were soon being shipped all over Europe by enterprising Alexandrian merchants. There was also at that time a brisk trade in local cadavers for somewhat the same purpose, though a woman writing to a friend in 1587 said that 'nue is not soe good as olde.'" He chuckled and the crowd, enjoying the display of wide-ranging knowledge and wit, chuckled with him.

At a signal from Stewart, the lights went out again and a new series of slides began. "So we had hopes of finding a tomb or burial site with at least partial mummification in a cave. Merlin was not supposed to be Christian, so he was less likely to have been in a churchyard or under a cathedral apse. We especially hoped for a mummy because in the last hundred years the science of paleopathology had been steadily advancing. We knew with a mummy we would have good chances of discovering from tissue remains what parasites and bacteria had afflicted Merlin during his lifetime and how he had died. We would read messages in his bones, the simplest and most basic being how big a man he had been, what kind of physique he had had, how long he had lived. But there were also ways to read between the lines: for example, was this a person from a violent society? Had he lived through a cruel childhood? What mistakes or accidents or diseases had he survived?" The grisly parade of mummy pictures continued.

"But first you needed the tomb!" called out Stevens.

The lights went on again.

"Exactly, Mr.—"

"Stevens. *Latin American Herald*."

"Ah, yes, Mr. Stevens. Good to have the Third World press here as well because what we eventually found affects all peoples, not just the English speaking. *And we found the tomb!*"

This was no surprise, though the hush the reporters fell into spoke more about their admiration for Stewart's ability to orchestrate. After all, the press conference had been called because the tomb had been discovered. Or at least something that Stewart claimed to be Merlin's tomb.

"I had been searching several possible sites for over ten years," Dr. Stewart said. "And then the unexpected occurred. If I were a religious man, I might venture to attach the word *miracle* to it. But we shall say, rather, that it was *serendipity*. I was on holiday in the fen country near a small marshy tidal river that bleeds off into the Bristol Channel. It was a working holiday, because I was on a picket line. Those particular fens were being drained and as an active member of the Royal Society for The Preservation of Birds, I was protesting the destruction of habitat. We had enough pickets and power and press reports to have extracted a promise from the government that the fens would be rebuilt once some system of proper drainage could be managed, for the river had become a breeding place of mutated tropical diseases since the influx of whole Ethiopian communities fleeing a half century of famine and war."

Stevens was scribbling madly now, his notes a hodge-podge of Spanish and English. Pritzkau, though, was sketching Stewart's head, emphasizing the bone structure until the drawing took on a kind of dark, wild, manic look.

"There was a local hill called the Tor which had figured in some of the early Arthurian material and, of course, the marsh was one of the possible sites of Ynis Avalonia, the Isle of Avalon. But when the draining began, the Tor, which had been partially under water on and off for centuries, rose up over that now bleak and blasted landscape like a great mountain. And at its foot, well below what had been the waterline, was a cave, a grotto. When I heard that news, I was there before sunrise with my cameras and a backpack of portable lights.

"The cavern entrance was small but the cave inside huge, as if it had been hollowed out. It was a virtual catacombs with small passages turning into large vaulted rooms, one after another. So mazelike was the whole thing, I was forced to chalk numbers and letters in the passages to guide myself. In fact, despite my precautions, I was lost for two days and nights, existing on the candy bars and apples I had fortunately carried with me.

"And then, almost as if by magic, on the third day I came upon a set of wooden doors ornately carved with runes. The doors had been so warped by the years of damp, it was easy to slip through them. But before I did, I managed to decipher the Latin motto carved in the upper arch."

The lights went out and a new slide came onto the screen. It took a second for the operator to focus it. When it was clear, the reporters could read the script around the lintel:

HIC JACET MERLINNUS

"Bingo!" whispered McNeil.

"As I entered the tomb, my torchlight dimmed and then went out as if being drained by some superior force, though probably the constant use over the two days had put paid to the batteries. I also carried a small wick lamp with me, and when I lit it and held it aloft, this is what I saw."

The next slide clicked quietly into place. The picture was of the well-lit interior of a cave, but even with all the lighting, the strange wooden casket in the center seemed a shadow.

McNeil mumbled something and Patti moved closer to him. "What did you say?" she asked.

"Just something, some gnomic saying I heard from somewhere."

"Which is. . . "

"To light a candle is to cast a shadow."

The casket was not a boxy, planed wood coffin but was an entire tree trunk lying on its side, the bark still in place. A second slide was a closer shot of the coffin. It filled the screen.

There were low murmurs around the room.

"It is a hollowed-out oak," Stewart said. "At first glance the bark seems all in one piece, but in fact part of it is not bark at all."

A new slide, an extreme close-up of the bark, replaced the last.

"The coffin was intricately locked and the lock was of incredibly wrought iron set in wood that was so carved it *looked* like bark." Using a light pointer, Stewart outlined the lock on the screen.

"I see it now," Pritzkau whispered, pointing. "Do you?"

Stevens leaned forward and shook his head.

"To the left of the pointer is a line, and that is the outermost edge of the lock and—"

"Got it."

The lights went on again. Squinting, the reporters scribbled notes to themselves in a variety of languages.

Stewart continued. "I mapped the route back to the room carefully and, when I emerged blinking in the bright light of a morning three days after I had first entered the cave, I was afire with the discovery. I was also tired, hungry, and extremely rank smelling."

"That he was!" It was the Prince of Wales. His timing was perfect, as the laughter from the audience proved.

Stewart stretched slightly and then continued. "We knew that the first thing to do was to make accurate maps of the entire catacombs. Then we needed to set lights and photograph the doors, rooms, the coffin, even before attempting to open the casket. It took me about six hours to assemble my team, with His Royal Highness' help, and it was only my long years of training that kept me from levering open the casket at once."

There was not a sound in the room as Stewart went on.

"We felt that it would be best to remove the tree to a laboratory and open it under better conditions. We had no idea what might be inside, you see, or in what shape. And ever mindful of the folklore surrounding such discoveries..." he hesitated, then added. "There is an old story about the opening of a tomb reputed to belong to Arthur and Guinevere which had long lain under a stone in Glastonbury marked HIC JACET ARTHURUS, REX QUONDUM, REX-QUE FUTURUS. For those of you whose Latin remains a bit rusty, that translates as Here lies Arthur, the once and future king."

"I'm sure glad he translated it for us," said Stevens.

"Actually," Mac said, "that plays a little cute with the translation. Literally it means Here lies Arthur, king way back when and also king in the future."

Chuckling, Patti said, "Latin still entact, Mac? You are a surprise."

"Parochial school," he answered. "Sister Maria Lucia and her famous ruler. You'd be even more surprised at the rest of the stuff locked up in my head."

Stewart had continued over the buzz of the reporters. "And when the monks opened the tomb, trying to make a bit of twelfth century tourist money on the event, all they discovered were bones and—so the story goes—a tress of hair."

"As 'yellow as golde'!" said the Prince of Wales suddenly.

"Yes. As 'yellow as golde.' But it turned to dust the moment it was touched. *Sic transit Guinevere.*"

Pritzkau sighed loudly and fluttered her lashes madly at Mac. "I so love a romantic story."

He laughed.

"We didn't want that or anything equally as tragic to happen to our remains," said Stewart. "So we decided to have everything trucked under the most careful conditions imaginable to a laboratory we had devised in a nearby town, Godney. Brought the mountain to Muhammad, so to speak."

A hand raised in the second row was recognized.

"Stemple, sir, of *Newsday*. You mean you actually brought all your instruments to Godney?"

"*Actually*, Mr. Stemple."

The room rocked with laughter, for that was the latest in-word brought over from America.

"We brought a portable X-ray machine for the bones and—if we were lucky—any soft tissue that might be revealed. And an electron microscope. Everything we need these days is portable. There was a big push in the nineties to make everything easy to carry so that actual field work— I use the word *actual* in its original sense—can be done *in situ*. But the grotto, analysis told us, was in danger of collapsing. The geological study indicated that serious cracks were developing hourly in the tomb room brought about by modern pollution and radical changes the draining had produced. We were forced to move to a stable site at once."

The prince was nodding his head vigorously.

"The reason we were able to move so quickly from the moment I found my way out of the cave was that His Royal Highness had also been in the area, leading the marchers against the draining program. We had had a luncheon date which I, lost in the caves, missed. His initial anger at my standing him up turned to concern when I could not be found. When I emerged several days later, it was into the arms of a rescue party he had mounted. It was he who secured us the place at Godney and the equipment in record time." Dr. Stewart nodded at the prince, who smiled through this recitation with the patient royal smile he had learned at his mother's knee.

"Our findings with the X-ray machine and the microscope I shall now sum up for you. If you have further technical questions, I shall be available to you all this week, either immediately following the conference or in the Godney laboratory."

Stevens said in an undertone to McNeil, "I can't see this being more than a couple of paragraphs at best. What a waste of time."

"You have no soul, Stevens," Mac said, laughing.

"I have no stomach—for long-winded dons."

"What we found was that inside the coffin was a mummy of an extremely tall, slim man. There were no appreciable Harris lines, or scars that showed interrupted growth on the bones, so the child who had grown into the man in the casket had been an unnaturally healthy child. Later on, under ultraviolet, the bones displayed the characteristic yellow fluorescence that reveals the mummy to contain a high level of naturally produced tetracycline. We sometimes find that in grain-reliant societies in damp climates a microbe called *streptomyce* is common. Nubian skeletons, for example, show high levels. If a person ingested enough of the microbe-infested grain, the natural tetracycline would confer a certain immunity to common diseases.

"We also discovered through X-rays that much soft tissue was still readable and, for those of you with a higher purient interest in Merlin and his love life, the man was uncircumcized. Of course circumcision was not common in England, except perhaps as a punishment to fit certain crimes. And then the cuts were made . . . well, rather further up."

The laughter that greeted this was rather subdued.

"We also discovered from the mummy's teeth and the residue of fecal material that he was most probably a vegetarian."

"Are you sure?"

"Mr. McNeil, isn't it?" Dr. Stewart said, his hand shading his eyes as he looked out into the audience.

"That's right."

"Well, Mr. McNeil, we are *pretty* sure. The scanning electron microscope can reveal typical patterns of wear on the teeth, wear that points to meat eating or bone gnawing or to habitual vegetarianism. As far as we can tell, for at least a good portion of his life, Merlin was a vegetarian. It is an educated guess, of course."

"Interesting," Mac said as he sat down.

"And the bones had one further wonderful surprise for us," Dr. Stewart continued. "The coccyx showed a strange elongated piece. It seems our mummy had a vestigial tail."

"Satan!" MacNeil said. "They called him a devil."

"One of the many rumors of Merlin's birth," Stewart

continued, "had been that he was an imp born of the mating between an incubus and a nun." He paused. "A man with a pronounced caudal appendage in that day and age would certainly be suspect. His own body fueled the stories."

The audience broke into spontaneous applause and McNeil turned, smiling, to Patti. "I *love* it!"

She smiled back.

"The scanning microscope also enables us to identify blood types within a given cell. Merlin—as we were already calling him with perfect equanimity—was AB negative which means he may well have killed his mother at birth. At the very least it was a difficult delivery, and given medical care at those times . . . He certainly comes from a different genetic type than the folk around him. And as he grew, with that extreme height and what seems, from the skull measurements we took, to be an elegant sloping forehead reminiscent of Chinese mandarin types, and the vestigial tail, coupled with his strange immunity to childhood disease, he must have appeared to his companions and neighbors both strange and wonderful. A miracle. And an alien."

Having said all this, Stewart reached over and unscrewed the microphone from its stand and walked with it toward the long table at which the Prince of Wales sat. For the first time the reporters noticed a wooden box about the size of a jewel casket on top of the table. The Prince's hands were cupped around each end. He was so obviously focused on the box that the audience responded in kind.

Dr. Stewart stopped in front of the table and half sat on it, gesturing with one hand toward the prince. "There was one last thing in Merlin's coffin, lying next to the mummy. It was a box, the box His Royal Highness is holding. As the box is small and hard to see from where you sit, let me describe it to you. It is made of oak and covered with high relief carvings that are a blend of Celtic knotwork, pictures, and runes. The pictures include a number of plants that are known for their magical or healing properties. On the left side, in the front, there is a sprig of mistletoe, on the right a picture of an acorn. On either end of the box is an apple tree—or at least a fruit tree of some sort. We are still trying to identify the other flora. On the back panel, lying down, is the skeleton of a man. As far as can be made out, the runes spell out an old Celtic saying, supposedly given as an answer to Alexander: 'I fear nothing lest the earth should split under me and the sky above me.' It is in keeping with the kind of prophetic utterances attributed to Merlin.

"When we X-rayed the box, it seemed to contain a fist-sized mass of soft tissue. The mummy itself had given us little clue to the reason for its death except perhaps the bones which indicated the man might have simply died of extreme old age. There remained, though, the matter of the curious long scar in the upper left quadrant of the chest. So we hypothesized that *after death* whoever laid out the body cut open the dead man's chest and removed his heart and that this was the mass we found in the carved box. Such a thing might have been a perfectly ordinary but—to us— unknown and unrecorded part of Celtic or Druidic ritual. Or it may have been that those who buried the man so feared his power that they felt separating his heart from his body was the only way in which they could be sure that he was truly dead. However, this thesis is complicated by the fact that instead of burning the heart or staking it or otherwise destroying it—as might be done to a true creature of the Dark—the sixth century morticians encased the heart in a special oak box carved with powerful runic devices.

"And they buried the casket next to the mummy and around the mummy's neck was hung a golden chain and a key.

"We do not know what it means."

As if on cue, the Prince of Wales stood and, holding the box, moved around to the front of the table. He cradled the box against his chest, and Dr. Stewart held the microphone before his mouth.

"It is our intention," the prince began, "to open the box in front of all of you so that whatever else we find in it will be seen as well by a hundred impartial and trained observers. We want you to report exactly what you see and hear. I suspect—*I* personally—not Dr. Stewart or any of the other scientists who have worked on this project, that something quite marvelous, quite extraordinary, quite *un*scientific or rather quite *beyond* science is about to happen."

Stevens leaned over and whispered to Pritzkau. "Isn't it true that he's the head of the Royal Theosophist Society?"

She nudged him into silence.

Stewart moved the microphone back to his own mouth. "I do not necessarily disagree with the prince. Our definitions of what constitutes scientific have always been somewhat—" he smiled at the prince who smiled back broadly, "—somewhat at odds with one another. But we both agree that what we have discovered about Merlin is already beyond our expectations. Now, before we open the casket containing the heart, are there any questions?"

Looking around, Stewart waited for hands to be raised but no one, it seemed, wished to hold up the show. There would be plenty of time for questions afterward.

"Then," the prince said and, when Stewart moved the microphone back so that he could be heard throughout the room, "then let us begin."

Holding the box with his left hand, he slipped a chain from around his neck with his right. Then he took the key attached to the chain and put it into the lock. With a *snick* amplified till it sounded like a gunshot, the key turned in the lock. As the audience watched in hushed anticipation, the lid of the box slowly creaked open by itself and a strange bone white light filled the room.

"Well, I'm still not sure what it all means beyond a couple of paragraphs. Maybe it belongs in the Arts and Leisure section," said Stevens moments later as they stood in line to leave the hall.

"What did you see?" asked McNeil carefully, his voice scarcely above a whisper.

"What we all saw," Stevens said. "A funny light coming from the back of the room and then the prince dropping the box and putting his hands up to his face. Then the lights going off for a second, then coming back on. Comic book stuff. And badly done at that. *We are not amused.*"

"Well, that's not what *I* saw," Pritzkau said.

"Of course it is."

"No. It isn't."

"What did you see, Patti. Please." McNeil's eyes narrowed and he leaned forward as if listening was an activity that suddenly took great physical energy.

"Well, the light of course, like Stevie says, only I thought it came *from* the box. And the prince doing his big act. But there was something more, something strange. I thought I saw a tree, as if it were projected from the box onto the screen. And then I smelled apple blossoms. The screen seemed, for a moment, to open as though it were a door that I could look through. That's where the tree was, behind the door. A whole orchard of apple trees in blossom. But it was just a momentary thing. A hallucination."

"Or a slide projected from the back of the screen," said Stevens. "We should check."

"*You* didn't see it," McNeil pointed out.

"I was watching the prince."

McNeil jammed his hands into his jacket pockets and stared at Patti. "Do you think—do you *really* think—the Prince of Wales would be party to such trickery?"

"What if he didn't know?" asked Stevens.

Patti shook her head. "What did you see, Mac?"

Stevens laughed. "Here it comes, lights, camera, action."

McNeil looked at the door ahead where very ordinary daylight was drifting in motes through the opening. From outside came the sound of chanting. The protestors were still at it.

"Come on, Mac. *I* told. What did you see?"

Could he tell them that at the moment the box had opened, the ceiling and walls of the meeting room had dropped away? That they were all suddenly standing within a circle of Corinthian pillars under a clear night sky. That as he watched, behind the pillars one by one the stars had begun to fall. Could he tell them? Or more to the point—would they believe?

"Light," he said. "I saw light. And darkness coming on." He bit his lip. Merlin had been known as a prophet, a soothsayer, equal to or better than Nostradamus. But the words of seers have always admitted to a certain ambiguity. He put his hands on Patti's shoulders and stared at her. For a moment his eyes were those of a dying man's. Then he laughed.

"My darlings," he said, "I have a sudden and over-whelming thirst. I want to make a toast to the earth under me and the sky above me. A toast to the arch-mage and what he has left us. A salute to Merlin: *ave magister*. Will you come?" If there was desperation in his voice, only he understood it. Desperation—and a last, wild, fierce, joyful grasping for life. He laughed again.

"What's so funny?" Patti and Steve asked together.

"Irony," he said. "The kind that only the Celtic mind can truly understand—or love."

After that he was silent and they had to follow him, still wondering, as he pushed through the door and into the aggressive light and the chantings of the crowd.

Well then, after many years had passed under many kings, Merlin the Briton was held famous in the world. He was a King and a prophet; to the proud people of the South Welsh he gave laws, and to the chieftains he prophesied the future."

—Vita Merlini
  by Geoffrey, of Monmouth

L'Envoi

Let all who trust in hidden power
   (The birth is in the stone)
Remember well the mage's hour:
   Find it,
   Make it,
   Bind it,
   Take it,
Touch magic, pass it on.